TRIN

THE
INVASION

ZACK SATRIANI

Hodder
Children's
Books

A division of Hachette Children's Books

Produced by Hothouse Fiction – www.hothousefiction.com

First published in Great Britain in 2013
by Hodder Children's Books

1

A Catalogue record for this book is available from the British Library

ISBN: 978 1 444 90662 2

Typeset in AGaramond Book by Avon DataSet Ltd,
Bidford on Avon, Warwickshire

Printed and bound in Great Britain by
CPI Group (UK) Ltd, Croydon, CR0 4YY

The paper and board used in this paperback by Hodder Children's Books
are natural recyclable products made from wood grown in
sustainable forests. The manufacturing processes conform to the
environmental regulations of the country of origin.

Hodder Children's Books
a division of Hachette Children's Books
338 Euston Road, London NW1 3BH
An Hachette UK company

www.hachette.co.uk

With special thanks to Adrian Bott

Prologue

Once, during a long and bitter war, the barren planet had been strategically important. Now the rusting wrecks of spaceships littered its bomb-blasted landscape, with bones and skulls lying among the debris.

The perfect place to build my finest creation. A planet where I will not be disturbed.

A man stood at the lip of an enormous crater, looking down. Below him, a monstrous construction was taking shape.

It was vaster than any temple or monument. As yet, the construction was unfinished. It was a mere skeleton, formed from thousands of metal girders twisted around with labyrinthine cables and pipes. But even in this unfinished state, it had a nightmarish quality to it, as if it were about to lurch out of the crater. Worst of all, it looked partly organic, as if it had been grown as well as built; a hideous merging of insect and machine.

Hundreds of thousands of greenish-yellow shapes, tiny from this far away, swarmed over it like fleshmites devouring a carcass. But they weren't feasting; these crawlers were *building*. They carried plasma welders, molecular binders, tekton spanners and a huge variety of electronic gadgets. The man barked an order into his wrist communicator, and a detachment of the creatures went seething off to the abandoned battlegrounds to fetch more materials. The hulks of crashed spaceships provided a constant supply of metal and components.

A column of the creatures went by, staggering under the weight of the girders they carried on their broad backs. They were like hybrids of spider and crab, with clawed limbs and long antennae. One stumbled under its load and fell, the girder crushing it with a sickening noise. The others ignored it. The next creature along gathered up the heavy load and carried on, leaving the fallen one twitching in the sand.

The man snapped at the creatures to pick up the pace.

Let the weak ones die. It helps me find the strongest specimens to clone.

Down in the crater, the creatures were welding

metal plates together. Sparks flew and hot metal flowed like blood.

The man smiled as the first of the outer plates was fitted into place on the construction. At last, the creation was growing a skin.

It is almost ready, the man thought to himself. *Soon it shall rise . . .*

1

Ayl sat cross-legged on an island of coral, looking out over calm shining waters as blue as his still-wet skin. His gills pulsed slowly in his neck as he breathed the air. All Aquanths could survive out of water, but it was a harsh, alien environment to them.

He would have been more comfortable practising his newfound telekinetic powers underwater. But then, doing tasks in *comfort* was no way to train his powers to become stronger. This had to be hard, or there was no point.

He lifted his hand and focused his willpower, forcing the water to move.

Instantly it obeyed him, surging and swelling in response to his commands. He gathered up a great rolling wave and stood in its path as it broke, letting the water splash down and over him.

Not long ago he had struggled to move that amount of water. Now it was as easy as swimming. *So what will*

I be able to do next? he thought. *Turn back tidal waves, or form moisture in the air into thunderclouds?*

Many times, Ayl had wondered what the limits of his power really were. The harder he pushed himself, the more amazed he became at what he could do. He didn't know whether it was possible, but he hoped that if he worked hard enough he might one day have the strength to move *himself* through space – and maybe even through time.

A vast shadow moved through the water by his feet. It was only a vambasha swimming past his island, one of the oldest ones he'd seen. The creatures were two-headed and shell-backed, covered with pearly nodules; ancient and peaceful ocean wanderers that grew larger than spaceships and filled the sea-lanes with their song.

A smile crossed Ayl's face as an idea came to him. Summoning up all his mental strength, he focused his attention on the area around the shadow and *flexed*.

A dome of water a hundred paces across steadily rose up like a surfacing bubble. The vambasha swished its flippers in the midst of it as Ayl strove to lift its surroundings out of the water in one go, trembling with the effort. Finally the dome became a ball of water, breaking from the surface completely.

Inside, the captive sea creature still swam calmly, unfazed by the rolling waves that now lay several paces below.

Ayl felt another presence. Someone had swum up behind him. If he turned to look, his concentration would break. He forced himself to focus.

The strain was beginning to hurt. His head pounding, Ayl gently rotated the sphere until the vambasha was pointing back the way it had come. Then, moving slowly so as not to shock it, he lowered the sphere back into the sea. He struggled to keep the whole mass of water from bursting free in one torrential gush.

Back below the surface, the vambasha flicked its flippers in what could have been amusement, and rocketed off under the waves. Ayl fell backwards and lay sprawled on the island's rocky surface, exhausted but triumphant.

'If you've finished rearranging the hapless wildlife of our planet, might I have a word?' said a voice behind him.

He laughed. 'Did you see that, Mother?'

'It was hard to miss,' said the Lady Moa, sitting down beside him. 'But I think the Current of Life would have given the vambasha wings if they had been meant to fly.' She laughed awkwardly. 'I wanted to ask . . .'

She hesitated, reluctant to say more.

'This is about the service at the temple, isn't it?' said Ayl.

'Yes. The thanksgiving service. I was hoping you'd lead a prayer.'

Six moons since it all happened, Ayl thought. Six short moons since the Nara-Karith were discovered on Zarix, where their leader, the rogue Bellori Sudor, had bred an army.

The threat had been stopped, but at a terrible cost. Ayl felt a lot more than six moons older. In his young life, he had experienced more violence and horror than most Aquanths ever saw.

'It would be my honour,' he said.

His mother gave him a look that said without words: *You sound like a Bellori.*

Ayl tried to explain. 'After Trade King Lial died, and then General Iccus . . . I saw it happen, so I ought to lead the prayers.'

'The service is to honour the dead, yes,' she said. 'But also to give thanks for six moons of peace.'

Ayl's mouth twisted ruefully. 'If it hadn't been for the dead, we wouldn't *have* any peace. The Bellori fought to save all of us.'

'And we Aquanths lent them our strength, breaking our sacred traditions to do so,' she reminded him.

They sat in silence for a moment.

She laid a cool hand on his shoulder and sighed. Suddenly she was just his mother again, and not the high priestess. 'Oh, Ayl. Must you always worry me so?'

'What have I done now?' Ayl asked.

'These powers you have . . . they are miraculous, and I truly believe they are a force for good. The Current of Life has blessed you with them.'

Ayl braced himself for the 'but'.

'But the way you're using them is wrong,' she said at last.

'The vambasha wasn't hurt, it wasn't even *upset*, it was enjoying itself!' he protested.

'It's not that! You are pushing yourself too hard, my son. Every day you come here, breathing the air, moving things around with your mind, working harder and harder! Then at night you're off to the temple archives, studying the ancient texts! When did you last spend any time with your friends? Poor Wan was half convinced you'd emigrated to Cantor!'

So *that* was what was eating her.

'I need to be as strong as I can possibly be,' he said quietly. 'And I thought you'd be happy that I'm studying.'

'I'd be happier if I knew why.'

Ayl thought for a long time before speaking again. 'I think I have a destiny. I can't prove it yet, but I'm certain. Dray and Keller and me – we're more than just friends. I think we have a higher purpose to serve. Danger is coming, and I need to be ready for it.' He clenched his fist. 'I need to be strong enough to fight it this time.'

'You truly believe in this destiny?' she asked.

'With all my heart.'

'Then *trust* to it,' she said. 'Don't try to outpace your fate. Be patient. Everything will be revealed when the time comes.' She stood up. 'Come back to the temple with me.'

She dived gracefully into the water, and Ayl followed.

The planet's surface was entirely composed of water, but beneath Aquanthis's waves lay a submerged lattice of coral and rock, where the Aquanths made their homes. Calm on the surface, a tangled labyrinth of shadows below . . . much like Ayl himself.

Not long afterward they reached Unity Temple,

a pyramid of white coral looming up from the murky seabed. It was swarming with activity as busy Aquanths darted everywhere like a school of frantic minnows.

The artisans' guild had created memorial sculptures from coral, which were being arranged along the far wall. They showed vague humanoid figures in postures that suggested grief and remembrance – covered faces, bowed heads, hands clasped in prayer. The artists hadn't made the figures look too much like any one of the Trinity System's three races. Ayl liked that. It suggested that the blue-skinned Aquanths, the armour-wearing Bellori and the pale Cantorians were similar, despite their very different appearances.

A strange mournful bellow sounded through the temple. The orchestra was tuning up, and a netherhorn player had just blown a practice note on a huge twisted instrument made of shell. Next, the notes of a xenoharp shivered through the water, making Ayl's spine prickle.

'Hey, podbrother! I'd just about forgotten what you looked like!' Wan came swimming over and clasped Ayl's hand warmly.

Ayl shook it and let it go. 'Well, here I am.'

'Come on over! We're sat up by the vestry. All the

11

old gang are here. Chel, Lok—'

'Ah, I wish I could,' Ayl said. 'My mother says I've got to lead a prayer. You know how she is.'

'Oh.' Wan's face fell.

'I'd better go work on it, figure out what to say. I think we'll be starting soon.'

'It's always *work* with you,' Wan said, unable to hide his disappointment. 'Go on. We'll catch you later.'

Ayl drifted off into a far corner, alone. His words to Wan had only been partly true. He already knew exactly what he wanted to say in the prayer, but the thought of spending time with his old group of friends didn't have the same appeal it once had. Ayl was glad that Wan and the others were prepared to accept him again now. After the way they'd cast him out before, when the violence in his memories had repelled them, it was a relief to be welcomed back. But he couldn't avoid the truth. He'd outgrown that group now. He'd seen so much, done so much . . .

Like fish in a pretty bowl, they had no idea what went on outside their limited world. It made him a little sad, but also a bit angry.

Only Dray and Keller had shared the same experiences as him.

They'll be here soon, Ayl thought, and excitement ran through him. Six moons! Would Keller still be making wisecracks, or would the burden of being Cantor's trade king have worn him down? Would he even recognize Dray after six moons as leader of the warlike Bellori people? She'd be back in her armour again . . .

Ayl looked back at Wan and the others laughing together over some joke. *If you only knew what Dray, Keller and I have been through together*, he thought. He ached to be with them again; the only other people in the whole system who understood.

'I will never understand these Aquanths,' grumbled General Tothin. 'Day and night they spout their platitudes about spirits of this and currents of that. They live in a child's fantasy world, filled with supernatural things. Living underwater for generations has turned their brains to mush.'

Dray, the commander-in-chief of the Bellori, looked down from her flagship's bridge at the waters of Aquanthis below them. She wondered how much more of this bellyaching she should tolerate. General Tothin had been grumbling ever since they had left Bellus, and he was not the only one.

13

Her Security Council had gathered on the bridge, flanking her to the left and right. All of them wore the famous Bellori armour: overlapping keratin plates, capable of resisting almost any weapon. Silhouetted against the peaceful blue orb of Aquanthis, they looked like a group of stern warrior gods . . . not that the Bellori had much time for gods, or the spiritual in general.

'They place so much faith in something they cannot even see,' agreed General Scraa. 'Only a fool would choose to trust some invisible force when he could have a good sword in his hand.'

'And now they invite us to their sodden world for a thanksgiving service!' grated old Brancur. 'To offer thanks for what, I ask? It was Bellori blood that bought their precious peace, not the daydreams of soft-hearted Aquanths.'

'Brancur, you drone on like a rotwasp,' snapped black-armoured General Vayne. 'Is this how we serve our commander-in-chief? By mocking our allies?'

Vayne rarely spoke, but when he did, he went straight to the point. Dray was glad to have his loyal support. Precious few of her generals could be counted on like he could.

Dray mentally kicked herself for not putting the

old warhorse Brancur out to pasture when she had the chance. He could have been prattling on to cadets at the Academy, filling their ears with stories of the glory of war. But no, she'd kept him on the council because her father had served under him.

'This entire trip is a waste of our time,' jeered General Mursh, the youngest and newest member of the council. 'We are Bellori! We should—'

'ENOUGH!' Dray roared, rounding on him.

General Mursh staggered back a step, startled. He tried to disguise it as a bow of respect, but everyone had seen it. General Vayne stopped him with a firm hand before he could back off any further.

'My General, I only meant—'

'The Aquanths are holding this ceremony to honour *my father*, and those who died with him!' She advanced on General Mursh, while the other members quietly backed away. 'General Iccus was your leader! Is honouring his memory a waste of your precious time?'

She heard Mursh swallow hard inside his helmet. 'No, General. I meant no offence.'

'No offence to *me*, perhaps, but you meant offence all right.' Dray raised her voice. 'All of you, listen. I will not say this again. The next one of you who shows disrespect to our Aquanth hosts, or to the ceremony of remembrance, will be assigned to Aquanthis for three full turns as special diplomatic envoy. That should teach you something about respect!'

She turned to leave, disgusted. 'Helmsman, prepare for the final approach to Aquanthis. All councillors, join me in the operations room. Not you, General Mursh! You can spend some of your precious time drafting a speech thanking the Aquanth high priestess for her kind invitation.'

Dray strode through the red-lit corridors towards the operations room. General Vayne walked alongside her in his gleaming black armour. The other councillors lagged behind, talking quietly among themselves.

She knew the operations room well. It was a dark space, almost like a theatre, where holographic images of the Trinity System were projected to show the deployment of Bellori ships and troops. For most of her life, she'd had to stay back at the room's edge while her father and his advisors made decisions about how best to protect the system. Now that responsibility was hers.

She directed the generals' attention to the slowly rotating image of the Trinity System, showing Bellus, Cantor and Aquanthis aligned around their sun. 'While we are on Aquanthis, we may be asked what we are doing to protect our allies against future attacks,' she explained. 'This is our answer; a thorough redeployment of our military strength. Use the time before the landing to familiarize yourselves with the details.'

'With respect, General, we are familiar with your strategy already,' said Scraa. 'Your plan to restructure the army has already been implemented. We made our views plain at the time.'

'As you commanded, the garrison on Bellus itself has been reduced to a mere tenth of its former size,' said Brancus in a dry voice, 'and our ships have been scattered throughout the Trinity System. Bellus now has almost no defence at all, save for the minefield. All planets are now defended, true – but at the cost of our own security.'

'Defending the *entire* system is our duty,' Dray reminded him.

'But how can we defend them, if we do not defend ourselves first?' Colonel Trosk asked. 'Since we first took to the stars, Bellus has never been left so exposed!'

'Maybe being exposed will help us to see clearly for once!' Dray yelled, finally out of patience. 'For our whole history we've been entrenched on our homeworld with only a few patrols into deep space, and where has that got us? If we hadn't been obsessed with guarding Bellus, we might have detected the Nara-Karith sooner and my father might still be alive now! By stationing the majority of the fleet near the outer rim, we stand a much better chance of detecting any invading force *before* they are on our doorstep.' She paused for breath, and remembered something a famous Bellori strategist had written long ago. '"We must be the broad shield, and not just the narrow sword."'

Trosk was unconvinced. 'A shield made from paper is no shield at all! With our forces spread so thin, how can we carry out an effective defence even if we *do* detect an invader?'

'General Iccus would never have left Bellus open to attack,' Brancur said boldly.

Even though their faces were hidden behind their helmets, Dray could hear loud mutters of agreement coming from some other members of the Security Council.

'General Iccus is *dead*,' she said in a voice of steel. 'I am in command here, not my father's ghost. If you dislike my leadership, feel free to resign!'

Dray turned away from her generals and took a moment to compose herself. She was grateful for the helmet that hid the annoyance on her face, as she pretended to analyse the data on the charts that lined the walls.

She felt exhausted, and there was still the Aquanth service to endure. For a moment, she felt a pang of doubt. What if the council members were right? With so many Bellori out on patrol, had she left Bellus itself too vulnerable?

No, she thought. *It is time for change. We must watch the skies, and be ready.*

The bowls of sweets hadn't lasted long, as Trade King Keller had expected. He sat in an armchair in the palace conservatory on Cantor, smiling as he watched happy, shouting children run back and forth through the ornamental fountains.

The conservatory was a glass dome where gorgeous alien plants thrived, crawling up growth rods in spirals of amber and scarlet, bursting into glowing blooms. The children's parents sat in armchairs of their own, facing Keller. The faces of these Cantorian citizens showed many emotions: suspicion; mistrust; cautious optimism.

'So that's where we'll be opening the new hospital,' Keller finished. 'Any other questions?'

'Why ask us up to the palace, Your Majesty?' said one man. 'I mean – there's nothing special about us.'

That's exactly why I wanted to ask you. 'Because you're Cantorians,' he said, 'and I want to hear what *you* think. I want you to speak your minds.'

'How did you choose us?' a woman asked suspiciously.

'By random lottery,' said Keller. 'With only one rule. Anyone whose income is higher than twenty credits a cycle was disqualified.' One of the men laughed at that.

'You want to know what the poor think, do you?' a stubble-chinned man said acidly. He hadn't spoken yet, Keller noted; he must have been saving this up. 'Well, I've got a question. Why don't you come down to one of the shanty towns in this city, eh? I could take you. Come and see what life is like less than half an hour away.'

'I've been there,' Keller said. 'And it made me sick. I saw people cooking food on chemical burners. Children drinking water from *fuel containers.*' The memory still stung him. 'I mean to fix that.'

The man folded his arms. 'Yeah, well, I *live* in one of them shanty towns. So tell me, Your Majesty.

How exactly are you planning to "fix" them? Wave a magic wand?'

'By building affordable housing for all workers,' Keller said. 'Paid for by a new tax on trading— Oh, krack. Excuse me. I think I'm wanted.' He stood up as two of his senior Trade Council members entered the room. 'Tyrus. Yall. Good morning.'

'Mummy, the trade king said "krack"!' said one of the children delightedly, running to her mother. 'He's rude! I like him.'

Tyrus, a bearded merchant, scowled at Keller with undisguised disapproval. 'It's time for us to leave for Aquanthis, Your Majesty.'

'I'm afraid this meeting is over,' Keller apologized to his guests, standing up. 'State business calls. But please stay and enjoy yourselves, and I hope to see you all again.' He turned and started walking towards the conservatory's arched southern gate, heading for his personal Mazakomi racing ship.

The route to the platform where Keller's ship was docked led over a skybridge. A slender architectural marvel, it arched over the royal gardens below. Groves of samthorn trees, thickets of shimmering blue cloudvine and beds of valleyblossom lay open to the rich sunshine.

Keller could see all the way to the royal hunting forest, with the white spire at its heart rising above the trees, marking the royal mausoleum where all the former trade kings were interred. *That spire cost a fortune*, he remembered. *It's completely indestructible, built to outlast any disaster.* His father lay beneath it now.

'Your father must be turning in his grave,' said Tyrus gruffly as he walked, following Keller's gaze. 'What were you thinking, making wild promises to the labouring classes? Affordable housing, did you say?' He snorted in contempt. 'They already have housing they can afford. There's a saying, you know – you can put a piggoth in a palace, and it'll turn it into a sty.'

'What my colleague *means* to say,' said Yall, giving Tyrus's shoulder a brisk double pat, 'is that the Trade Council is upset.'

'Then take them this message from me, their trade king,' said Keller. ' "Get over it." '

'Ah ha ha,' said Yall. 'Your Majesty is most witty. Bluntly, then: the increased taxes you have levied upon Cantor's traders to pay for your schemes have made a lot of important people very angry.'

'He thinks he can take money out of the merchants'

pockets and just give it away,' muttered Tyrus.

'My people need my help, and I'm helping them,' Keller said. 'Is that so hard for the Trade Council to grasp?'

'You, sir, are the *Trade* King of Cantor, just as your father was *trade* king before you!' exploded Tyrus. 'In case you're having trouble remembering, your job description is helpfully written directly under a picture of your face across banners, flags and coins all over the blasted planet!' He fished a coin out of his pocket. It showed Keller looking imperious, strong chin jutting out and dark hair swept back. 'See? "Trade King Keller", it says! Well, not from where I'm standing!'

'I think what my colleague is driving at,' Yall said, 'is that a trade king's first duty is to generate commercial profit for his planet, not act as a charity.'

'Some of us still want to earn a living!' shouted Tyrus.

Keller wondered if he was trying to do too much too fast. Tyrus was right about his father, anyway. He would never have taxed trading like Keller had. Cantor was a planet of merchants, above all else. There would be nothing but grief from the Trade Council for as long as he kept up these reforms. Maybe he was trying to fix the unfixable. Maybe it just wasn't worth it . . .

No, he thought. *I've been to those slums. I've seen those people suffering with my own eyes and I can't let it go on.* He had to do what was *right*, never mind what the Trade Council might think.

They reached Keller's sleek Mazakomi racing ship. The young trade king performed a lap of the craft, carrying out routine safety checks, while Tyrus and Yall grumbled by the main doors. Keller felt irritated to think of the two of them in his favourite ship. They'd probably bend his ear all the way to Aquanthis.

'And this Aquanth thanksgiving business is a waste of taxpayers' money, too,' Tyrus groused. 'Bunch of superstitious claptrap if you ask me.'

'It's not like there aren't other planets that he could visit,' Yall agreed. 'The galactic trade guilds have been crying out for an audience with the trade king! Think of the revenue that could generate! Gods forbid we should try to put money *into* the treasury instead of giving it away.'

'Since you've obviously forgotten,' Keller called over his shoulder as he made his way up the steps to the craft, 'the Bellori and Aquanths aren't just important allies and neighbours, they're Cantor's best *customers* as well! Can't you see how important it is for us to keep strong relations with them?'

Tyrus opened his mouth to say something but Keller didn't want to hear it. 'I know you'd hoped for a lift, but I'm afraid this flight is fully booked, gentlemen,' he said, stepping through the entrance and turning to face them. 'We shall discuss this further on my return.' With that he punched the hatch control and the door slid down with a reassuring thud.

Keller grinned and fired up the Mazakomi. Through the window of the cockpit he saw Tyrus and Yall running for cover, not wanting to be caught under the engines as it took off.

He pressed a red button and the ship rose into the air on jets of blue flame.

Keller engaged the main thrust, relishing the sudden tug of G-forces. His heart pounded as the ship gathered speed and his grip tightened on the vibrating controls. The ground fell away below him like a discarded shroud. They couldn't reach him now. He was *free*, soaring wild and bright through the sky, screaming high above the treetops and toward the white clouds high above. He laughed aloud from sheer exhilaration.

'Waa-hoo!' he hollered. No doubt Tyrus would carp and moan, and call him irresponsible. But he'd deal with that later. For now, there was just the freedom of the open skies.

He knew he ought to lay in a course for Aquanthis, but he couldn't resist having some fun first. He looped the loop, leaving a trail of exhaust behind him like graffiti on the blue sky.

2

'On final approach now, General,' called the Bellori helmsman. 'Touchdown in sixty clicks.'

General Mursh peered at a nearby console. 'Something's wrong. The beacon's transmitting, but there's no landing pad. They don't expect us to land on water, do they?'

Dray had anticipated this. 'We'll be meeting the Aquanths in their own element, under the surface. The flagship can be placed in hover mode until we return. As you were, helmsman.'

The endless oceans of Aquanthis rolled past beneath them, clearly visible through the command deck windows. It could not have been more different from Bellus, which was as dry and rocky as the slopes of a volcano. Nobody but a Bellori would ever understand the feelings their homeworld inspired in them. It was as harsh and brutal as they were, and they would give their last drop of blood to defend it.

Dray wondered how anyone could ever love Aquanthis. Ayl had often said it held hidden beauty, but this immense watery nothingness filled her with a sense of sorrow. She imagined floundering in it forever, adrift, never reaching dry land again. The Aquanths insisted it was beautiful, but where was the beauty in this blue-green expanse?

'Landing party, attach your breathing modules,' she ordered.

Dray and her council passed around bulky devices fitted with clear hose attachments and fist-sized bulbous power cells. They clicked into place on the Bellori armour suits, fitting over the air vents on the sides of the neck. Now the armour was watertight and had an artificial gill system, able to convert oxygen from the water into breathable air.

'Ten clicks until landing,' the helmsman said. The sea was surging up to meet them. 'Activating repulsor fields *now*.'

Invisible to the eye, massive fields of force bloomed out from the underside of the *Astyanax*. Impossibly graceful for something so vast, the flagship descended ever more slowly until it came to a standstill only paces above the ocean's surface. Like a city suspended in the air it hovered silently, the mighty Bellori engines keeping it from dropping that final distance. Waves danced in the great blanket of shadow beneath it.

Dray realized she had been holding her breath, and let it go.

'Commendable landing, helmsman. Diplomatic party, come with me to exit ramp nine. We can meet—'

The distant hum of jets suddenly rose to a deafening shriek. A missile? Dray ran to the viewscreen.

Next moment there was a titanic boom and splash, as if a meteorite had struck the ocean just a few paces from the flagship. Dray glanced up in alarm, just in time to see green seawater sluice over the viewports. Then the flagship tilted wildly as the wave pounded it.

The Bellori staggered, some falling to the floor in a clatter of armour, others grabbing safety rails. Dray caught hold of a console and pulled herself to her feet.

The ship tilted the other way, helpless now in the water's grasp. The viewports were slathered with sea creatures and strands of weed. Tentacled Aquanth life-forms struggled in the backwash.

Krack, Dray thought, *we're under attack!*

* * *

The button marked EJECT had been flashing a brilliant red. Keller had fought the controls, struggling to peel away from the water's surface – and then he'd hit it. The impact had shaken him around like a lifepod in a storm.

Now, as the water boiled around his still-plunging ship, a thought flashed across his stunned mind: *I'm still alive*.

Then: *Good. Let's keep it that way*.

He hit the full braking flaps, hoping to slow the ship even further.

Just then, a massive jolt flung him back in his seat and a long grinding screech of metal on rock told him he had hit the sea bed. All he could do was hang on until the violent shaking stopped, praying the ship's hull wouldn't tear open.

Eventually, the Mazakomi racing ship came to a standstill.

It was dark under the sea. Only the cockpit lights provided any illumination.

'That,' Keller admitted out loud, 'could have gone better.'

The ship didn't answer him.

Keller thought about it, then added, 'Water landings aren't easy to pull off at the best of times,

OK? So I'm out of practice. Give me a break.'

The ship remained silent.

Keller checked the readouts, hoping the ship wasn't too beaten up. They showed some damage to the underside of the hull, and the ship's com-link seemed to have gone dead, but nothing that couldn't be fixed. Keller gave a low whistle. At the speed he had been going, he was lucky not to have shot straight through the planet and out the other side. With a guilty start, he saw the waves he'd made had all but capsized the Bellori flagship.

Well, he thought with a shrug, *that's one way to announce my arrival!* Without a working com-link, there was no other way to tell the Aquanths that the Trade King of Cantor had arrived.

The computer readout showed that Unity Temple was just ahead on the ocean floor. Sediment began to swirl around the cockpit of the Mazakomi in clouds and something with long spindly legs went scooting past.

He popped open a storage locker to reveal a top-of-the-range scuba suit. For a planet that had started out as mostly desert, Cantor had a lot of deluxe water parks – all water imported from Aquanthis, of course – and a trade king could afford the very best gear.

The suit felt considerably looser than it had the last time Keller had worn it. *I guess that's one advantage of being too busy to eat snacks*, thought Keller. He pulled the breathing mask down over his dark hair and opened up the inner hatch. He stood in the narrow airlock space and sealed the hatch behind him, then unfastened the outer doors. The cool dark waters of Aquanthis flooded over him.

He kicked himself away from the ship and began to swim. The crash landing had stirred up a lot of ocean debris. Sand and weed fragments swirled around him so thickly he could barely see his hand in front of his face. He turned on the suit's head-mounted light, but the beam just made the snowstorm of particles seem thick as fog.

'Now, which way to the temple?' Keller asked himself aloud. 'I guess I'll just have to ask someone for directions.' His voice sounded tinny and strange in the enclosed space of the breather mask.

He froze. Something was moving through the murk, a dark shape bigger than he was. It began swimming in his direction. Keller wished he had a weapon, or at least some sort of bodyguard. There was nobody around to help him. Didn't the Aquanths have any kind of security force? Of course not, they were all pacifists. They probably just stood there and said prayers while banesharks bit their arms and legs off.

The thing was nearly upon him. It loomed through the dark, levelling a weapon at him. So, at least it was intelligent. Maybe he could reason with it.

Keller braced himself to fight this Aquanth predator, whatever it was. In the full glare of his lamp, it looked almost like an armoured Bellori warrior.

Wait. It *was* an armoured Bellori warrior. That was a k-gun it was pointing at him.

Keller's breath caught in his throat as he saw the ornamental crest on the helmet. Only one Bellori was entitled to wear that. The one who commanded all the others.

'Hello, Dray.'

'Nice landing,' Dray said. Her sarcastic voice resounded from her helmet, amplified by its internal speakers. 'Have you considered a career as a guided missile?'

'Lovely to see you, too,' said Keller. 'Would you mind pointing that thing somewhere else?'

Dray returned her k-gun to its mount on her back. 'Stand down!' she called behind her. 'There's no attack. Just the Trade King of Cantor having some trouble with his ship.'

The other Bellori delegates swam into view behind Dray. 'I suggest we escort the trade king to the ceremony,' one of them said icily. 'It might help to avoid . . . diplomatic incidents.'

Dray nodded. 'This way.'

Keller swam behind Dray, following the light from her helmet. As they emerged from the cloud of sea-bed muck his ship had stirred up, he got his first clear look at the *real* Aquanthis – the world below the water's surface.

It was, quite simply, stunning. They were swimming over the edge of a vast cliff, which proved to be the near side of a stupendous undersea canyon encrusted all over with structures. Lights glittered in the sides and floor of the canyon where the Aquanths had built their dwelling places. They weren't made from bricks or blocks like Cantorian houses; they seemed to have been shaped from the rock itself.

Dray led the group down the canyon's slopes towards the sparkling Aquanth capital city. Fish darted in schools above its spires like flocks of birds, and huge fronds of colourful kelp rose high above the rooftops. Keller wondered why the Aquanths even needed roofs to their houses, since rain could hardly be a problem here. Then he saw that many of the rooftops were in fact gardens, shimmering with phosphorescent plants and ornamental coral sculptures.

Dray was still swimming confidently ahead. Keller watched her armoured legs power through the water, finding it hard to believe that inside the keratin plates was a girl the same age as him with blonde hair and an atheletic figure. He suddenly felt giddy and something fluttered nervously in his stomach.

It'll be the change in pressure, he thought.

When the first group of Aquanths had silently left the temple after setting up the memorial statues, Ayl hadn't been too worried. Perhaps they were just hired artists, and they had no reason to stay.

But then the group who had installed the ornamental sea-frond displays had left, along with the caterers, the shell arrangers and the musicians' helpers. Even Wan and his group of friends had glided out of the door, once they'd finished laying out the lights on the altar.

Ayl was now almost alone in the temple. Only the orchestra still stood waiting, along with his mother, the high priestess.

'Isn't the ceremony due to start any moment now?'

he asked her, confused. 'It hasn't been cancelled, has it? Shouldn't Keller and Dray be here by now?'

'The Bellori are on their way,' his mother told him.

'So why is everybody leaving?' Ayl asked, confused.

His mother sighed heavily. 'I think I just told you why.'

Ayl realized what she was saying. 'But . . . they can't just leave! It's a sacred ceremony . . . they ought to attend!'

Perhaps you should tell them so, his mother thought to him.

Ayl sent his own thoughts out in an open broadcast. Ordinarily, Aquanths wouldn't have ever done this except in an emergency; it was like shouting, but more so. A whole city could hear one person.

Where are you? he broadcasted. *The ceremony is about to start.*

He caught whispers of thought in response, tinged with guilt, disgust, even hostility.

You cannot make us sit in the temple with the Bellori! They are primitive warmongers!

We have done our part. The temple is prepared. Now let us depart in peace.

We don't need to be there, do we? Our high priestess can speak for us, can't she?

36

Ayl forced himself to forgive his own people for their ignorance. They haven't seen what I've seen, he told himself. They've never fought alongside the Bellori, nor been honoured by them.

I never thought Aquanths could be so ungrateful, he told them. *The Bellori have given us a great and precious gift, and this is how you repay them?*

Gift? came the puzzled response. *What gift have they given us?*

The gift of life itself, Ayl explained. *The fallen Bellori gave their lives defending us. The living Bellori devote their own lives to protecting all of the Trinity System, including our fragile world. We owe our very lives to them. Tell me now: which of you is willing to throw that gift of life back in their faces?*

Ayl waited.

Slowly, with Wan leading them, the Aquanths began to swim back into Unity Temple. Ayl watched as they took their seats, trying to mask the shame on their faces.

His mother's voice echoed softly in his mind. *I am proud of you, Ayl. That was well spoken indeed.*

Just then, an armoured Bellori swam through the main archway, closely followed by a somewhat ungainly Cantorian in a scuba suit. Other Bellori followed after them, their armoured bodies casting dark shadows against the pale coral of the temple walls.

Many of the gathered Aquanths glanced away as the bulkily clad warriors made their way among them, sitting down on the temple benches. The sight of the Bellori seemed to offend them.

Ayl shook his head. He made straight for Dray and Keller and gathered them both up in a warm embrace.

'Welcome to Aquanthis,' he told them so that everyone could hear. 'We're honoured to have you with us.' He grinned and added in a whisper, 'And I'm very glad to see you, too, my friends.'

3

'As our three worlds move into close alignment on the same side of our sun, the three peoples of Trinity gather together in peace,' announced the high priestess. 'The service of thanksgiving and remembrance will now begin.'

Sitting with Keller on one side and General Vayne on the other, Dray felt uncomfortable and awkward. The Aquanths clearly didn't want the Bellori here, except for Ayl, of course, and she was sure the Bellori group would rather have been out hunting raptaurs and emberwolves on the great dust plains of Bellus. It all seemed pointless.

And yet, as the orchestra began to play long mournful notes that sounded as if some mighty mother was grieving for her lost children, and the high priestess recited a prayer for the spirits of the departed, she found herself slowly but surely drawn into it.

'May the souls of the fallen rejoin the Current of

Life, and journey ever onward toward unity with the One, even as all rivers flow towards the sea . . .'

Dray wondered what her father's soul was doing now. Was the spirit of General Iccus looking down on her proudly? Did he even have a soul? Dray tried to imagine him transparent and ghostly, but it was absurd. He'd been the most solid thing in her life. The old man had never mentioned belief in any sort of afterlife – not to her, anyway. Had he talked to his male friends? Colonel Ruskot? With a pang, she realized how little she'd known him.

They had hardly ever talked about anything beyond her training, the army, and the orders of the day. No wonder she'd been desperate for him to recognize her. It had meant the world to her when he'd entrusted her with the mission to kill Sudor – the mission she had failed. That was the last time she'd ever seen him alive.

I understand now, Father, she wanted to say. *Why you barely spoke to me, even though I was your daughter. It made me so bitter and sad. I thought you were ashamed of me, but now I'm a leader myself, I know the truth. The pressure of command demands that you stay focused at all times. A whole world depends on you and you can never show them weakness. You HAVE to be hard as titanium.*

She wished he was in front of her now, so she could

ask him about her strategy. Had she left Bellus too exposed? He would have known what to do, surely. And now it was too late.

The sound of Ayl's voice brought her momentarily back to herself. 'I'd like you all to join me now as we pray for peace. Whether you honour the Current of Life, or even if you have no spiritual leaning at all, let's hope we never again see such times of violence.'

It was a very different Ayl than the one she'd first met. He was so confident now – at ease in his own skin. He'd fought with his inner demons and come out the other side, scarred but whole, a citizen of a bigger universe now. She noted with approval how he'd subtly included the sceptical Bellori in his prayer.

Could she ever complete that journey for herself? Dray had no answer to that. All her life she'd lived in hope of one day earning her father's respect. Now he was gone forever, how would she ever know if she was good enough?

Lost in her own thoughts, she didn't notice everyone else standing up. They were joining hands.

Keller nudged her. Startled, she stood up and saw he was holding out his hand to her.

She took it in her armoured fist, feeling more awkward than ever. Ayl began to chant, and everyone else joined in. As Keller's hand gripped hers, Dray was glad that he couldn't see her face inside her helmet. He would have teased her for blushing, she knew.

'Great service, Blue,' Keller told Ayl afterwards.

'Yes,' Dray said solemnly. 'It was very, um . . . spiritual.'

'Glad you thought so!' Ayl grinned. 'If you liked that, then you'll love what I've got to show you next.'

'The Hydroball stadium?' asked Keller excitedly.

'Better than that. The grand library of Aquanthis!'

'Wow,' said Keller. 'I'm yawning in excitement already.'

'No, seriously. This is worth seeing. Come on.' He swam ahead of them, leading them through the weed-straggled spires and encrusted domes of the Aquanth city. 'It's only a few channels from here.'

'Channels? Are those like streets?' Keller asked, avoiding the soft purple fronds of a hovering jellyurchin the size of a cargo skimmer. It seemed to be eating barnacles off a wall.

'No streets on Aquanthis,' Ayl said with a laugh, remembering how strange and confining the streets of Cantor had seemed to him. 'We don't need them. Channels are . . . well, they're like agreed paths that everyone takes. Some go through tunnels in the rock, some through water. Don't worry about the jellyurchin, it's harmless. It's just cleaning up.'

Their route took them under the blank, steady gaze of a row of immense statues, eerie in the underwater half-light. They all held strange objects: one a horn, one a book, another a complicated measuring implement.

'Are they your gods?' Dray asked suspiciously.

'No! They're the *lahreow*. Great teachers of the Aquanth people,' Ayl explained. In truth it was a little more complicated than that – the *lahreow* were believed to guide individual Aquanths through visions and dreams, depending on fate and the movement of the stars – but Keller and Dray didn't need to know that. 'The library's down this next slope.'

'So where are all the shops?' asked Keller.

'We didn't even know what shops *were* until we met you people,' Ayl explained. 'Aquanths believe that everyone should give according to his ability, and take according to what he needs.'

'No disrespect, Blue, but that's crazy.'

'Not when you're telepathic,' Ayl said softly. 'You understand other people's needs a lot better when you can feel their hunger or pain like it was yours. When

43

you live in each other's heads all the time, sharing is the only way.'

'Your homes aren't very well protected,' Dray observed. 'Most of those houses don't even have doors, let alone locks. How do you defend yourselves?'

'Against what?' Ayl asked. 'Thieves? Everyone has everything they need. Predators? We just use telepathy to placate them. We're kind of used to peace here.'

'Too used to it,' Dray called from behind him. She was struggling to keep up, and Keller wasn't doing much better.

Ayl laughed and did a graceful somersault through the water. 'Get a move on, you two! Makes a change for me to be the one out in front!'

The library loomed before them, a pillared structure like an ancient mausoleum. It was so eroded and coral-infested, it looked as if it were merging back into the rock. 'This building's one of the oldest on the whole planet,' Ayl said in quiet respect. 'The library's been here for hundreds of thousands of turns. And the artefact we're here to see is even older.'

'The books must be a bit soggy by now,' Keller muttered.

'Oh, please,' Ayl rolled his eyes. 'All the modern

records are stored on data crystals. The oldest ones are carved on stone tablets. And then there's this.'

Ayl could hardly contain his excitement as he led them to a dim recess at the back of the library. A solitary green crystal lit an alcove, in which a strange stone slab had been mounted. It showed three interlocking circles, with an inscription gouged deeply into the surface beneath.

'The legends say this tablet fell from the stars, millions of turns ago. It says "Three become one" in ancient proto-Aquanthean,' Ayl explained. He waited breathlessly for their reaction, but all Dray and Keller did was to look at each other then back at him.

'And?' Keller said.

'It's about us!' Ayl exploded. 'It's got to be! Everything I've always felt about us having a destiny, the pattern of fate that links us together – this proves it!' How could the two of them be so blind?

Keller's face was blank behind his scuba mask. Dray stared a moment longer, then turned and swam angrily towards the door.

'I don't have time for riddles!' her voice hissed from her suit. 'I've got problems enough of my own to deal with. Real-life problems!'

* * *

Keller had to laugh at Dray's blustering. 'Have you, now? I'll make a deal with you. Trade your so-called problems for mine. How about that? Try being Trade King of Cantor for a cycle, and you'll soon know what a real headache feels like!'

'Oh, you've actually taken office now, have you?' Dray's voice had an edge to it like a *scratha* knife. 'You've been so quiet on the subject of military spending, I thought maybe you were on holiday! "He'll answer me when he's home from his pleasure cruise," I thought.'

'I was *going* to answer those coms,' Keller said through his teeth. 'I've had a lot on my plate lately. At least your generals aren't always trying to conspire against each other like my Trade Council!'

'Well, let's sort it *now*, seeing as we're both here. We need to deploy Bellori ships to patrol outlying Cantorian trading posts, and we need you to fund their operating costs.'

'What is this, a protection racket?' Keller snapped. Behind him, Ayl was still looking gloomily at his precious stone tablet.

'Security needs to be stepped up across the whole outer rim!'

'And conveniently, you're the only security provider

in the system. So, what, I'll just traipse back to my Trade Council and tell them I'm putting taxes up *yet again*, shall I, so I can fund an increased Bellori presence that, surprise surprise, the *Bellori* have told me we need? My head won't just be on coins if I try that – it'll be outside the palace gates. On a spike!'

'We Bellori are supposed to be your military advisors. Maybe you should listen to us?'

Keller folded his arms. 'Go on then, military genius. Tell me why I need armed ships to protect a few outlying trade posts, with Sudor banished from the system and the Nara-Karith wiped out? What are you afraid of? Is this what passes for bravery on Bellus nowadays? For a planet of legendary warriors, you're acting like a bunch of nervous old women!'

He got ready to enjoy Dray's furious response, but Ayl interjected before she could speak. 'She might be right, Keller. I'm not sure the danger is gone.'

'Look, Blue,' Keller said in as friendly a voice as he could, 'I know you've got good reason to be jumpy. I mean, who wouldn't be after all you've been through, right? But you have to understand, if there *was* anything dangerous still out there, the Bellori patrols would have picked up on it. They've got the best deep-space scanning equipment money can buy. I should know – it was my money that bought it.'

'I just *know*, all right?' Ayl yelled in sudden anger. 'You can be as condescending as you like, but I *know*. Something big is going to happen, and soon. I've had this feeling before.' He gave Keller a cold glare. 'And I've never been wrong yet.'

Suddenly, a shrill, frantic beeping began to sound, disturbingly out of place in the peaceful library.

It was coming from Dray's wrist-com.

4

'General Vayne here.'

Vayne, with something to say for once? Oh krack, this must be important. 'Sentinel post Vanguard 6 is reporting a massive build-up of wormhole energies on the edge of the Trinity System.'

Dray knew what that meant. Because of the oddities of space travel, wormhole energies appeared *before* the craft itself warped into an area, like the bow-wave of an approaching ship. The bigger the incoming ship, the more energy.

'Massive, you say?'

'Yes. Something's heading our way, General. Something huge.'

'Have you determined what its target is?' She tried to keep her voice from trembling.

'We can't. Not until it arrives. That should be any moment now. All we know is that the energy levels are off the scale.'

'I'll head back to the *Astyanax* right away!' She closed the com and saw Keller and Ayl watching her with worried faces. 'Something's come up,' she said abruptly. 'I need to get back to my people, *now*.'

She began swimming as hard as she could, heading back through the library's outer halls. Aquanths bending over data crystals saw her floundering through the water and sped away, darting like fish out of the path of a baneshark.

Why doesn't this armour have a powered swim-turbine built in? she thought angrily. It was meant to protect her, but it was just slowing her down. A terrible feeling was stirring in the depths of her mind. *I left Bellus unprotected, and now something's going to attack us.*

Ayl and Keller were swimming alongside her. Ayl made it look so easy, and even Keller looked graceful in the water. *It's not fair. I'm stronger than both of them put together. I'm the athlete, not them! Why can't I just slip through the water like they do?*

'Dray, let me help,' Ayl said. He put his hand to his mouth and made a strange, shrill noise like a whistle that went shivering through the gloomy building.

'What was *that* for?' she asked.

'Wait and see.'

The next moment, a bluish-grey shape rocketed out

of the darkness like a torpedo. It was fish-like, but it had smooth skin instead of scales and merriment twinkled in its amber eyes. There was a silvery ornamental cap fitted to its head, and the powerful tail that lashed the waters was ringed with fluorescent jewelled bands.

It's a sacred beast of Aquanthis, Dray realized. She'd seen images of these creatures on Aquanth banners and statues, but usually they had had Aquanths riding on their backs.

'I can't ride that!' she protested.

'You don't have to. Just hold on to one of his fins. You too, Keller.' Ayl patted the creature's flank affectionately. 'Hold on tight. I'll tell him to bring you back to the temple.'

One moment, Ayl was frowning in concentration. The next, Dray was hanging on for dear life as the creature launched itself through the water. She could feel the buffeting force of its tail threatening to shake her loose, but she tightened her grip. The creature bucked and thrashed like something driven clean out of its wits, towing them along at breakneck speed.

Across from her, Keller was yelling a muffled 'Yahoooo!' The bubbles from his mask swept behind them like a silvery streamer in the wind. Even Ayl was struggling to keep up with them now. Dray looked down at the Aquanth city flying past only paces below. Some Aquanths looked up from their rooftop gardens and shook their fists in disapproval. That just made the ride all the sweeter for her.

'That was amazing,' she admitted when the creature finally drew up outside the temple. 'I'll have to take you riding on the plains of Bellus some time. This thing is fun, but it's tame compared to riding a Shanti dragon.'

'I'll hold you to that,' Ayl said with a smile.

Dray's contingent were waiting for her on the steps, with the Aquanths giving them a wide berth. 'The object has warped into the system,' General Vayne said, getting straight to the point as he always did.

'Then what is it? What are we dealing with?'

'We have no visual data as yet,' said General Scraa tensely. 'All we know is it's travelling at speeds far higher than any ship we've previously encountered, and we have to assume it's hostile. We tried to get as much data as we could, but the one probe ship that was in range was destroyed instantly. There's a chance the next outpost station might spot it.'

That was a manned probe, Dray thought, feeling

sick. 'They must have been able to tell its course! Where was this thing heading?'

'It started to move just after warping in, we couldn't—'

Dray's wrist-com was beeping again. 'Yes?'

She knew what the faint, distant voice would say before it even spoke. 'General Dray, this is outpost station Halberd 21 on emergency broadcast. We have its vector. The unidentified craft is heading towards *Bellus*. Repeat, the target is—'

The soldier's last words were drowned in a hiss of static.

Ayl looked on in horror as Dray began to bellow commands. 'Generals, assemble your squads. We are *leaving*! Fall back to the *Astyanax* and prepare for immediate return to Bellus! Go! Go! GO!'

Sheer chaos broke out. The Aquanths went rocketing away from the temple like startled tadpoles as the Bellori mustered in the outer courtyard. They yelled to one another, arming their weapons and thumping fists against armour as they prepared for war.

Ayl could hear the telepathic messages humming all around him as the news spread. *A hostile craft in the system, heading for Bellus! Moving faster than anything ever seen before! A probe and an outpost destroyed already! Who have the Bellori managed to anger now?* And then a thought so callous and stupid it made him grit his teeth: *If you ask me, those Bellori had it coming, the way they swagger about.*

Once the squads were assembled, there were no goodbyes. The Bellori swam as one, moving up from the temple towards the surface. Ayl swam after them, with Keller close behind. *I'm not letting Dray face this alone*, Ayl thought.

The flagship's boarding ramp was already lowered into the water. The Bellori clambered out and stood there in a dripping row as Dray ordered them to carry out a swift check of their weapons.

'What's she doing?' Ayl hissed to Keller. 'There's no time for a weapons check!'

'It's routine,' Keller said grimly. 'They *have* to check their weapons. Part of the whole Bellori honour code.'

'Arm the fusion torpedoes!' Dray yelled as her boots clanked up the boarding ramp. 'Prepare for immediate take-off. Send a transmission to *all*, repeat *all* Bellori forces in the system: return to Bellus immediately!'

All over the flagship, gun ports hummed open

and gigantic turrets emerged from behind armoured shutters. Fusion torpedoes clanged into their firing tubes. The Bellori were going to war.

Ayl heard the Aquanths thinking to one another: *And they wonder why we don't want them here on our world! Always looking for a fight, those Bellori. Thank the merciful Fates they didn't try to start one here.*

He climbed on to the boarding ramp and stood watching the chaos with calm eyes. He didn't panic. Everything was falling into place, just as he had foreseen.

Dray turned on him angrily. 'Blue, what are you doing? Off my ship. We need to launch!'

'I'm coming with you,' he told her. 'So's Keller. It's our destiny. Three standing together as one.'

'Sounds good to me,' Keller said with a shrug.

'Out of the question!' Dray raged. 'One, you'd just slow us down, and two, there's no reason to risk your lives as well as ours! If you want to get yourselves killed, do it somewhere I won't have to watch!' She turned her back on them.

'Dray,' Keller replied calmly. 'Remember what happened last time Blue talked like this? And the time before that? He *does* see things coming. Maybe just this once, we should take him seriously?'

She stopped in her tracks. 'Fine. Come aboard, find somewhere out of the way and stay there. I'm fighting for my homeworld, and I don't intend to lose.' She punched a control beside the ramp strut, and the ramp began to rise. Ayl quickly scrambled aboard.

'I'm going to fetch my ship,' Keller said. 'Be right back!' He ran to the end of the rising ramp, dived off the edge and went under.

'We won't wait for you,' Dray growled after him. The ramp finished its ascent and clamped shut.

Ayl settled into an uncomfortable seat. He focused his mind, sending a telepathic message to his mother and to Wan. *I'm going to Bellus with Keller and Dray. I'm sorry to leave so suddenly, but I can't fight destiny. Some currents are too strong to swim against; you have to let them carry you.*

His mother thought back. *You wanted to be strong enough for this moment when it came, and all too soon it is upon us. I pray you will find the strength you need.*

Wan was more direct. *Stay safe, podbrother. I'll pray for you.*

'Docking clearance granted, Cantorian. Proceed.'

The Bellori helmsman hadn't bothered to address him as 'Your Majesty', but right now Keller had much more pressing things to worry about. He guided his racing ship up inside the underbelly of the Bellori flagship and waited for the robotic locking arms to secure it before shutting down the engine.

He had just finished changing back into his regular clothes when he felt the whole ship shudder.

'We've launched,' he said to the Bellori technician in charge of the hangar bay. 'Next stop, good old Bellus.' The technician saluted awkwardly.

I just hope Bellus is still there, he thought, calling the elevator to take him to the bridge.

On the bridge he found Dray looking up at the ship's viewscreen, along with Ayl and the brooding Bellori generals. The screen showed a map of the Trinity System, with Aquanthis, Cantor and Bellus lined up almost perfectly on the same side of the sun. That mass of tiny dots surrounding Bellus like a halo were the famous minefield.

A large, flashing blob moving rapidly towards Bellus was flagged as 'UNKNOWN'. The word gave Keller chills. When he saw how fast it was moving, horror crawled up his spine.

'What *is* that?' he breathed.

Nobody answered him. *They don't know any more than I do.*

'Full speed, helmsman!' Dray barked. 'We have to get to Bellus before that thing does!'

'The minefield should slow it down,' General Scraa said confidently.

'It'll slow us down, too,' General Mursh reminded him. 'We can't just charge into our own minefield. We have to avoid the mines, and that means taking our time.'

A decent pilot could weave his way through them easily enough, Keller thought, glancing darkly at the Bellori helmsman.

'More speed!' Dray yelled, banging her fist on a console in frustration.

A crude-looking metal sphere bristling with long, narrow spikes went hurtling past the ship. Keller felt cold as he saw just how close it had come. *A child could have avoided that!*

'We've entered the minefield, General,' said the helmsman. 'Carrying out standard evasive manoeuvres . . . dropping speed to recommended safety limit.'

Keller's palms itched as he watched the man work the controls. *To hell with that by-the-book stuff! I could get us through this minefield with all the afterburners going.*

'Can't we go any faster?' Dray was sounding hoarse now.

'The unknown vessel has entered the minefield,' pointed out General Vayne. 'Its speed is twice our own.'

'How is that even possible?' said Dray. 'I need more speed. Forget the safety limit!'

They were in the thick of it now. Mines were volleying past, and even at reduced speed the helmsman had to fight to keep the ship clear of them.

'General,' grated Brancus, 'there is no point in destroying our own flagship! We have to reach Bellus intact even if that ship gets there before we do!'

'Which it will,' said General Vayne. 'Look! It's halfway through the minefield already.'

Keller glanced at Ayl. The Aquanth had always hated flying, and was bound to be a nervous wreck with all this going on. But to Keller's surprise, his friend had his eyes closed and seemed to be meditating serenely.

'Frequent flyer now, aren't you, Blue?' he said with a nervous laugh.

'Set the shields to maximum!' Dray was shouting. 'We'll just smash our way through!'

'Boosting shields will take power away from the drive,' the helmsman said helplessly. 'I can get us to Bellus quickly, or safely – but not both!'

'Then I'll find us a pilot who can!' She marched to the helm and physically lifted the helmsman out of his seat. 'Keller? Take us home!'

'Finally!' Keller cracked his knuckles and took the helm. 'OK. Engineering, give me all the thrust you've got. Hold on tight, people.'

Keller flew like he'd never flown before. In his hands, the immense Bellori flagship handled like a graceful stunt flyer. He piled on the thrust, trusting to his hair-trigger instincts to zip and weave around the mines.

'A single impact,' warned General Tothin, 'and we'll all be eating vacuum.'

The mines came zooming out of the darkness of space as thick as hailstones in a hurricane. Sweat ran down Keller's forehead as he swerved and swerved again. Everyone on the bridge held on to the security rails and safety straps. Soon the red-orange sphere of Bellus was dead ahead, and only a few mines remained.

'Unknown object almost out of the minefield,' said Vayne in a voice of ice.

'Come on, Keller,' Dray urged. 'You can do it!'

Keller swore as a vast cluster of mines appeared right in front of them. He threw the flagship into a corkscrew spin, angling its wings to slice through the narrow gap between the mines. From somewhere behind came a huge, buffeting explosion as the mines collided with one another.

We can ride the shockwave out of here! Keller thought, hanging on to the helmsman's yoke as it vibrated in his grasp. *Play it cool, make it look like you meant to do that . . .*

'We're clear of the mines!' cheered one of the generals.

General Vayne shook his head. 'But too late. Look.'

On the scanner, the alien craft was already entering the atmosphere of Bellus. Bellori surface-to-air missiles immediately fired at the craft, but it deflected the rockets as if the blasts were merely firecrackers.

A host of tiny dots burst from the craft and spread out in a wide array, heading off in all directions, moving to encompass the whole planet.

'Warheads?' gasped General Tothin.

'No,' one of the technicians called up from his scanner. 'They're not warheads – they're pods, holding life-forms! It's dropping troops over the whole planet!'

'Put that ship on the main screen,' Dray said flatly. 'Let's see what we're dealing with.'

Everyone on the bridge gasped as the first image of the intruder filled the viewscreen. It was a ship, but like nothing Keller had ever seen before.

Larger than a city, it had eight immense articulated limbs and a central core that bristled with fearsome weapons. The whole thing looked as if it were somehow alive, about to latch on to the surface of Bellus like a monstrous parasite.

It came down in a gigantic cloud of dust, not far from a flat-topped pyramidal structure.

'That's the Security Council's command bunker!' Dray told him.

But Keller was still staring at the colossal ship. He swallowed hard. 'Um, is it just me, or does that look a lot like a Nara-Karith?'

5

Dray couldn't believe what she was looking at. The craft was easily ten times bigger than her own flagship. *Even if we'd caught up to it, would we have stood a chance?*

The ship's eight limbs came down on to the rocky surface of Bellus – and *through* it. They sank deep, drilling down like claws sinking into flesh.

Cold fury choked up Dray's throat. *That's my planet! I'll tear you off Bellus, you stinking heap of scrap!* Her generals gathered around the viewscreen, staring up at the monstrosity.

'What are we waiting for?' barked General Mursh. 'We have pulson turrets on this ship, don't we? General Dray, we should begin a strafing run at once. Let's blast that ugly thing off the face of our planet.'

'Pulson fire is prone to ricochet, and could damage the command bunker as well,' General Vayne observed. 'Our adversary chose his landing site intelligently.'

'Then what would you counsel?' Mursh demanded.

'Land assault. Deploy the troops to attack that thing's underbelly. Let them cut their way inside it with plasma torches. Find out what we're dealing with.'

'Infantry against an armoured ship?' said Scraa. 'They'd be cut to ribbons.'

'We should evacuate the command bunker and trigger the self-destruct, and turn that thing into a smoking crater!' roared Brancus.

I have to say something, Dray thought, but she couldn't speak. All she could think of was how utterly responsible she felt. *Why didn't I listen to them? I was so sure I knew best . . . and I left my own homeworld unguarded!*

The mammoth ship lay there like a great hand slapping her in the face, a crude insult to every worthy Bellori instinct she'd ever felt. To have been invaded so *completely* . . . she felt violated and humiliated all at once. *I did this. I tried to do what was best for the whole system, and I let my own people down.*

Behind her visor, her face was wet with hot tears. Now her generals were looking at her, waiting for her to speak. She couldn't. The moment she opened her mouth, they would know how weak she was. They would know she blamed herself for this. And she would never be able to live it down.

Keller saved her without even knowing it. 'What *is* that thing?' he wondered aloud, and suddenly everyone on the bridge was looking at him instead.

Dray swallowed and swallowed again, tasting the salt of her own tears, forcing herself to be calm. She bit down on the inside of her mouth until the pain brought her to her senses.

When she finally spoke, her voice was thick but steady. 'I'm not sure, Keller. But I have my suspicions. And I intend to find out.'

Keller didn't like the sound of Dray's voice. Had she been *crying* inside that helmet of hers? *She should have given me the controls sooner. We might have blown that thing out of the sky before it even had a chance to land.*

'I do *not* intend to waste lives in a rash attack,' Dray announced. 'For all we know, that vessel can shrug off anything in our arsenals. Bombing is out of the question, too. It's dug itself in deep. We could harm Bellus more than that ship has harmed it.'

Keller wondered what harm a *planet* could possibly suffer, especially one that seemed made of rocks and dust, but he kept quiet.

'We need information,' Dray said. 'That means reconnaissance. We need to send a scout ship and find out what we're dealing with.'

'That ship has already destroyed one probe and a listening post!' yelled General Scraa. 'What more does it need to do, General, before you conclude that it is a threat and must be destroyed?'

An uproar of voices joined in. All the generals in the room seemed to agree with Scraa, and were thumping their chests to hammer home the point. Keller looked over at Ayl again, but the Aquanth was still watching calmly, as if he'd seen this a thousand times before. There was something unsettling about his detached serenity, Keller decided. He was acting almost *holy* these days.

Dray roared for silence and banged her fist on the tabletop. Keller had long since got used to the Bellori habit of trying to make more noise than everyone else, but the sound still made him jolt.

'There was a time when I would have jumped recklessly into battle,' Dray growled. 'Not any longer. There is no honour in dying like an idiot.'

'We have been challenged and we must fight!' howled Brancus. 'It is the Bellori way!'

'Any fool can fight! Any fool can *die*! A true Bellori

warrior fights wisely. I learned that the hard way, on the battlefield.' Dray's voice took on an icy edge. 'Maybe you have all been armchair generals for too long.'

Keller cleared his throat. 'General Dray, can I suggest we scout out the alien ship using my Mazakomi racing craft?' He couldn't resist a grin of pride. 'It's smaller than any of the fighters you've got here on the flagship. Much faster, too.'

'That thing? A flimsy toy. You might as well go scouting in a paper dart!' snorted General Scraa.

'Maybe if we had an Aquanth with us who could create a cloaking field,' Keller said, winking at Ayl, 'that would ensure we survive the trip!'

General Scraa was silent.

'I'd be honoured,' Ayl said, moving to stand shoulder to shoulder with Keller. 'Even if it does mean more of your insane flying.'

Dray just nodded. 'We're in your debt, Trade King Keller. Let's go. General Vayne, you have command of the bridge until I return.'

'You can't possibly be going yourself, General!' General Scraa said in disbelief. 'The risk—'

'The commander-in-chief of the Bellori asks nothing of her people that she would not be willing to do herself,' said Dray, walking from the room. 'It is the Bellori way.'

The elevator took them down to the hangar, where they all climbed into Keller's craft. He checked the readouts and was pleased to see the Bellori had made repairs and refuelled it, though they hadn't done anything about the scratched paintwork. There were Bellori priorities for you.

The little racing ship emerged from the flagship's underside and, in a roar of blue jets, went powering through space. Keller took them to the edge of Bellus's atmosphere and angled down. Even at this distance the alien ship was clearly visible, a dark blot like a scab on the planet's surface.

'Bring us in close, Keller,' Dray said. 'We need a good look.'

'Roger that!'

'Should I cloak the ship?' Ayl wondered aloud.

'Yes!' Dray answered him instantly.

Keller took them down through Bellus's outer atmosphere, plunging through rusty-coloured clouds and towards mountains that looked like insect mounds from this height. Winds howled mournfully around the racing ship, and Keller silently prayed the Bellori repairs would hold up.

He brought the ship down, finally levelling off as close to the ground as he dared to fly. The landscape of Bellus went rocketing past them, a panorama of rocks and sand as gritty as its warrior people. The scanner registered the spider-like craft up ahead.

'There it is. Krack, look at that thing. It's *huge*.'

The craft loomed on the horizon, an impossible shape that seemed too colossal to be real. As he brought them in closer, he saw how intricately built it was. The way the panels fitted together, the articulation of the legs, the almost organic quality it had . . . it was obscene, but he couldn't help being impressed by it.

'Whoever built that thing really knew what they were doing,' he muttered to himself.

'Bring us in close to that leg!' Dray said. 'I need to see as much as I can!'

The leg loomed like a skyscraper beside their ship. Thousands of cables twined across it, looking like mechanical veins. Keller didn't know whether to feel amazed or ill.

'Look!' Dray yelled, pointing. Oval hatches were opening at the base of the leg, like pores expanding in skin. Keller marvelled at the technology.

'The other legs are opening, too!' Ayl said, pressing

himself up to the clear polymer of the racer's canopy. 'Every one of those legs is an exit!'

For what? Keller thought, but he didn't have to wonder for long. Familiar insectile shapes were pouring out of the hatchways and marching in long columns across the landscape.

'Nara-Karith!' Dray said.

Under his breath, Keller muttered, 'Here we go *again . . .*'

The Nara-Karith came marching out in endless widening streams, heading in eight different directions across Bellus. *They're going to lay waste to the entire planet*, Ayl thought. *I knew they were in there the moment I saw that ship. I could sense them.*

'Keep circling, Keller. I want a good view of this,' Dray said. She pointed her k-gun at the cockpit window.

'What are you doing?' asked Keller.

'Recording on my gun cam,' she replied. 'My people are going to tear those bugs apart.'

Ayl felt uneasy. The spider-like creatures, with whiplike antennae and crushing pincers, were marching out in military formation, row after endless row.

'Where are all the Bellori?' Ayl asked anxiously. 'I can't see anything but rocks!'

'Keep watching,' Dray said.

One of the Nara-Karith columns was nearing the command bunker, a pentagonal structure of grey plascrete surrounded by a perimeter wall. Ayl wondered how the Bellori could possibly have left it so undefended. Nothing stood in the Nara-Karith's way but a plain of reddish dust and a field of jagged rocks. Were there mines under the sand? Robotic drones?

The Nara-Karith marched closer. They were almost at the bunker's outer wall.

'Now they're in range,' Dray said with cold satisfaction, sighting down her k-gun. 'Watch and learn, boys. *This* is why we're the warriors of the Trinity System.'

Light shimmered from the rocks. Seemingly out of nowhere, Bellori soldiers appeared, becoming visible against the craggy background. They hastily set up tripod-mounted cannons that were so festooned with blades and spikes they could have been used as spears to hunt behemoths.

'Camouflage nets!' Dray said. 'Not as powerful as your cloaking field, but we have a lot more of them!'

The Nara-Karith didn't stop or even slow down.

The Bellori plasma cannons opened fire, sending a barrage of red pulses into the oncoming host. There was a rumble of explosions, and the front rank of Nara-Karith vanished in a spattering of body parts.

Keller let out a low appreciative whistle as he brought the ship back around. 'That's some firepower.'

'There may be a lot more of them, but we have bigger guns,' Dray remarked. 'At this rate it shouldn't take us too long to mop up.'

Down below, the plasma cannons were firing continuously now, their barrels glowing white-hot. Bellori soldiers had to keep feeding fresh ammo discs into them.

Two groups of Nara-Karith, each one led by a huge mutated-looking leader, broke away from each side of the main horde and tried to come around in a pincer movement. A Bellori commander yelled an order, and his men peppered the aliens with frag grenades, tearing the columns apart. Ayl saw one of the Nara-Karith leaders ripped almost in two. The other was simply obliterated, turned to a fine yellow mist.

'Stupid bugs,' Dray mocked. 'Thought you'd just help yourselves to my planet, did you? We'll wipe you out.'

Despite the confidence in her voice, Ayl couldn't

help noticing her hands. She was cracking her knuckles again and again. *She only does that when she's nervous.*

The situation didn't look good to him, no matter what Dray might think. The Nara-Karith were *seething* out of the ship now like woodlice from under a lifted rock, spreading out over the planet in a skittering carpet of insectile bodies. The plasma cannons kept on pounding, but the oncoming aliens just trod the shattered corpses of their former comrades without the slightest hesitation.

They have no fear, no emotion of any kind at all. They don't care if they lose ten thousand warriors, so long as one of them makes it through . . .

The bodies were piled thick on the ground, but the oncoming army had almost reached the plasma cannon emplacements. Even Ayl could see that those hefty slow-tracking weapons would be no use in a hand-to-hand fight. The Bellori warriors were unclipping k-guns from their backs, setting bayonets and arming grenades.

'Still coming?' Dray murmured. 'Then we'll give you what you've come for. A quick death.'

Her soldiers were hurriedly arranging themselves into formation, the front ranks kneeling, the rear ranks taking aim.

'That's right,' Dray hissed. 'Give them everything you've got!

Ayl braced himself for the sound of k-guns. To him, that unmistakable *whip-bang* sound would always mean one thing: the moment he'd killed for the very first time. He remembered how another creature had died in front of him. With every muscle tense, he waited for the first gunshot.

But he heard only silence.

6

The Nara-Karith were almost within striking distance of the Bellori, and yet the k-guns weren't firing. *It's some sort of trap, a subterfuge*, Keller thought. *It's got to be.*

Then his mouth fell open in silent amazement. The first rank of Bellori soldiers gently lowered their k-guns to the ground. Not a single shot was fired. The smoke from the plasma cannons still drifted across the battlefield, but the only noise was the quiet anticipatory clicking of Nara-Karith pincers as they marched to surround the Bellori.

The soldiers left their weapons lying there and stepped away from them. Then they lifted their arms over their heads in a gesture that could only mean one thing, no matter which planet you were from.

There was a slow ripping noise behind his shoulder. Dray was gripping the back of his seat so hard her fingers were tearing through the deluxe fabric.

'What are they doing?' she screamed at the top of her voice. 'What are they *doing*?'

'They're surrendering,' Keller said hollowly.

'They can't be, they'd never do that, not under my command . . .' She began to prime her weapons. 'Keller! Land this ship right now! I'm going to go and take care of the situation *personally*!'

'Not going to happen, Dray. This was a reconnaissance mission. Fast in, fast out.'

'Land! That's an order!'

'I don't take orders from you! I'm not one of your grunts!' Keller regretted those angry words the moment they left his lips, but it was too late to take them back.

'I ordered this scouting mission, it's under my authority! Land!'

'Not happening! Use some common sense! What could you possibly achieve against that many Nara-Karith?' Keller nodded down to where the seething mass was now completely encircling the Bellori. Not one of the soliders offered any resistance at all.

There was a scrape of metal on metal. Suddenly Dray was holding a *trunga* knife, a short sharp blade the Bellori used to skin wild raptaurs.

'Dray, don't do this,' Ayl warned. 'Remember, we're friends—'

A snort of derision was his only answer. Dray wrapped an arm around Keller's seat and pressed the knife blade to his throat. He felt the keen edge bite into his flesh, and smelled the mineral tang of the oil she used to clean it.

If Dray's grip shifted by as much as a millipace, Keller's throat would open up like a skinsuit unzipping. In that frozen moment, time seemed to slow. As if powerful forces were deadlocked with one another, neither of them moved a muscle.

'You might want to put that thing away,' he said evenly. 'If we hit turbulence, there's going to be a hell of a mess.'

'This is your last warning, Keller,' she replied in a voice that froze his blood. 'Land.'

'It's your funeral,' he said grimly, conceding defeat. The spell was broken. He felt her fingers relax a little, enough for him to steer the craft down towards the rocky surface of Bellus.

With luck, he'd find a concealed landing site where Ayl could drop the cloaking field. He could still feel the cold of the knife at his throat, but couldn't tell if she was still holding it there.

Ayl's serenity was beginning to fray at the edges.

They were much closer to the Nara-Karith now, and the aliens' thoughts were roaring through his mind. He had never faced so many, not even on the asteroid. This was a fully-fledged army, thousands upon thousands of the things. Their thoughts hammered at his consciousness like a swarm of rotwasps buffeting a window.

It took all his mental strength to keep them at bay and maintain the cloaking field at the same time. He telepathically carved out a silent hollow for himself, an eye in the storm, and focused on it. For a moment he envied Keller and Dray, who were deaf to the Nara-Karith's constant chittering. They would never know how this felt, the agony of thousands of malevolent voices raging through your mind.

Gather arms. Gather arms. Gather arms, they repeated over and over again. Their minds seemed encased in mental armour, unlike the Nara-Karith he had faced before. His own thoughts couldn't penetrate it. There was no chance of controlling any of them – and what was worse, they seemed to be controlling the Bellori.

As Keller searched for a safe landing site, Ayl and Dray watched the battle unfold through the cockpit window. The Bellori stood like statues, not even speaking a word of defiance, as the Nara-Karith scooped up their weapons in their clawed arms. From huge tripod-mounted cannons to handheld k-pistols, they helped themselves to everything.

Dray had seen enough. She vaulted out of her chair and stood by the exit hatch, k-gun at the ready. Keller remained in the pilot's seat alongside Ayl, watching the Nara-Karith at their plundering.

'It's like the first day of Cantor's winter sales,' he said bitterly, rubbing his neck. Nobody laughed.

At least they aren't slaughtering the Bellori soldiers, Ayl thought. But horrible though the thought was, he had to wonder why they weren't doing it. Why take an enemy's weapon if you didn't mean to kill him with it?

Loaded up with stolen weapons, the Nara-Karith began to march back to the spaceship. *Store arms, store arms*, went the pounding chant in their minds.

'They can't do this,' Dray was yelling. 'I won't let them do this.'

'Wait! Reinforcements are coming!' Ayl told her excitedly. 'They'll take care of it!'

A fresh platoon of Bellori soldiers was spilling out of the main security bunker. They ran at the Nara-Karith, opening fire as they did so. The sound of their k-guns blasting the aliens to pieces echoed across the plain like distant fireworks.

Dray didn't pause in her preparations. She clipped a vibroblade bayonet on to the end of her k-gun and slung a loop of grenades over her shoulder.

Ayl turned back to the battle. To his horror, the second wave of Bellori suddenly froze in position just as they were about to engage the enemy. One moment they were running, the next they just stood there locked in place, like empty suits of armour. *What are the Nara-Karith doing to them? They're paralysed!*

A telepathic wave boomed out from the Nara-Karith. *Drop your weapons.*

The Bellori did as they were ordered, letting rifles and pistols fall clattering to the ground.

'How horrible,' Ayl whispered in disgust. It was mental domination, the use of telepathy to overcome another person's free will. To the Aquanths, it was the most terrible crime imaginable, so dreadful it did not even have a name. They only called it *The Abomination*.

'Why's this taking so long?' Dray yelled.

'Touching down now!' Keller yelled back. 'I'm setting us down behind that row of hills. It should be just out of sight of the main command bunker.'

The racing ship landed and the door opened with a

hiss of hydraulics. Dray ignored the ladder and jumped all the way down to the ground.

'Don't go!' Ayl screamed. 'You don't know what you're walking into!'

But she was already out and running across the red sand.

The harsh soil of her homeworld crunched beneath her boots. Dray felt stronger for it. To her, touching the soil of Bellus was always like finding a missing piece of her own self. She was back where she belonged, ready to fight, and good luck to anyone who got in her way.

She reached the low row of hills that lay between her and the enemy, hiding the ship from view. She would crouch among the rocks at the top, then pick off the largest of the Nara-Karith from behind cover. Then, when the others realized she was there, she'd mow down as many as she could.

She set off up the hill. This was her hunting ground. She felt she knew every rocky valley, every ashen plain, every scree slope and perilous mountainside. She could survive out here without aid; she knew where to find secret stockpiles of water, the best places to defend against ground or air assault, the camouflaged ammunition dumps.

The Nara-Karith could never hope to know Bellus as well as she did. That was some small comfort, at least. She could use the terrain against them – trap them in valleys too sheer to escape, lead them into sinkholes or over crusts of deceptively fragile rock where a misstep could send you plunging through into the hot lava beneath . . .

But even that tiny flame of comfort flickered and died in her as she pulled herself over the crest of the hill and looked down to see a column of Nara-Karith filing past at the base. They were scrambling over the sharp, jagged terrain as if they were born to it. Nothing seemed to slow them down at all.

Down by the command centre the Bellori soldiers were standing immobile, docile as herd beasts. *Fight!* she wanted to scream. *What's wrong with you?* To hell with sniping from range. She activated her vibroblade bayonet and braced herself to charge.

Before she could move, from out of the command bunker came yet another platoon of Bellori soldiers. They had to move around in a wide arc to avoid shooting on their own comrades, but as soon as they had a clear line of fire they let rip.

Dray clenched her fist in satisfaction as the insect-like creatures shattered and burst, mown down in scores by the pounding rifles.

The Nara-Karith were still advancing! Dray didn't understand. *Stupid bugs, why are they marching right into a hail of rifle fire?*

Disgusting gouts of yellow blood flew through the air and a severed limb whistled over her head, but the aliens didn't stop or even slow down. The uninjured ones just climbed over the bodies of the dead and kept going.

She heard the platoon commander yell an order to charge. One moment, the Bellori soldiers were running as one toward the alien ranks, laying down rifle fire as they went. Next moment, they simply *stopped*, like machines turned off by a single switch.

'No!' Dray roared inside her helmet.

The k-guns the soldiers had been brandishing fell to the ground. Their other weapons soon followed. They surrendered *everything*. Grenades, razordiscs, even their *trunga* knives. The Nara-Karith helped themselves to the weapons, gathering up as much as they could carry before scurrying back to their ship.

Anger surged through Dray's body like molten metal. A red mist filled her brain. How DARE they surrender? They were traitors, milkblooded cowards, every one of them.

'You NEVER surrender!' she screamed, flecking the inside of her visor with spittle. 'You fight and you die *with honour*!'

The faces of the dead flashed in her mind: *Colonel Ruskot. Commander Zhora. Lieutenant Rokar. My father.* They had all gone the way a Bellori should go, fighting to their last breath. She would not see their memory betrayed.

Her body was moving, driven by pure rage. She was running on warrior instincts now, giving no thought to her actions. She was like a berserker, all the old Bellori blood foaming up in her veins. She vaulted over the rock ledge and ran at the Nara-Karith.

'Cowards!' she shrieked. *I'll show them how a true Bellori can fight!*

One Bellori warrior against thousands of Nara-Karith. Those were good odds. As she ran, she raised her k-gun and let out a long war-scream like the howl of a raptaur.

7

Keller's throat was stinging from the knife scratch, but it didn't hurt half as badly as his pride. *How dare she pull a knife on me!* He was Trade King of Cantor, not some scrappy Bellori recruit for Dray to order about. Well, once she was safely back on board the ship – *his* ship – he'd have a few well-chosen words with her.

'Next time she wants to go on a scouting mission, she can use her own kracking ship,' he muttered. 'She'll be back all right. Once she sees close up what's happening to the other Bellori, she'll come running.'

But then, through the cockpit window, he saw Dray go running *towards* the Nara-Karith, brandishing her k-gun and screaming at the top of her voice. She vanished over the rock ridge.

He sat bolt upright. 'What in the name of Cantor is she thinking?' he wondered aloud.

'I'm not sure she's thinking at all,' Ayl said nervously.

'Ship,' said Keller, 'patch into Dray's gun cam! Show us what's happening!'

A jolting image appeared on the scanner screen. Dray was running down the slope of the rust-coloured hill, acting like a one-woman army. The Nara-Karith at the bottom had noticed her now, and were wheeling around to face her. *They'll tear her to pieces!*

It was insane, but it was also the bravest thing he'd ever seen. General Dray, like General Iccus before her, was laying down her life for her people.

While he sat safely in his ship, watching it from a distance.

Keller muttered a curse and pulled his Z-42 pulse rifle from under the front seat. 'I guess I'd better give her a hand,' he said, fitting an ammunition cartridge. 'I mean, *someone* has to pull her backside out of the firing line, and it might as well be me.'

'No!' Ayl warned, grabbing his shoulder. 'You won't get anywhere against them. Look.'

The image through the gun cam was steady now. Like all the other Bellori, Dray had suddenly frozen to the spot. Keller and Ayl watched the Nara-Karith teeming around her, clutching at her body with their nipping pincers, tugging her treasured weapons away.

The view lurched and swivelled as a Nara-Karith

grabbed Dray's k-gun. Now they could see her through her own gun cam, standing still as a statue.

'What's she doing?' Keller gasped.

'It's mind control!' Ayl managed to burst out. 'Somehow those Nara-Karith have learned to use telepathy as a weapon. They're reprogramming the Bellori, forcing them to see the Nara-Karith as their masters.'

'But the Bellori have the strongest willpower of anyone!' Keller protested. 'You can't break a Bellori – can you?'

'Look. Do you need any more proof than that?' Ayl asked, sounding sick.

The view through the gun cam was blurry and lopsided, but there was no doubt about what it showed. The Bellori were removing their armour.

Keller felt horror trickle like icewater down his spine. The Bellori armour defined their identity. To remove it was unthinkable, a taboo most of them would sooner die than breach. Yet they were lifting off helmets and unbuckling chest plates while the Nara-Karith looked on.

'So they force them to take their armour off, and then they kill them in cold blood while they can't resist?' Keller said in sudden panic. 'Stinking bugs. I wish we'd wiped them all out on that asteroid!'

Dray twisted her helmet and lifted it off her head. Through the gun cam, Keller caught a glimpse of her pale face, framed by fair hair. It made him catch his breath in horror. Her grey eyes were glazed and her mouth hung open, as if she were already dead. A walking corpse.

'I'm not leaving her to be butchered by those bugs,' he told Ayl. 'We've got to do something!'

'Stay close to me,' Ayl said, summoning up all his mental strength. 'This will only work if we stick together.'

'Got it!'

Ayl transferred the cloaking field from the ship to Keller and himself. Back when he was first discovering his powers, this would have been a challenge to make his head spin. Nowadays it was as easy as jumping in a lake.

'We're invisible,' he said. 'Let's go.'

Keller hesitated. 'I can still fight from inside this shield of yours, right?'

Ayl grimaced. 'Yeah, you can shoot through it if you have to. But they'll get suspicious if they just start dying and they can't see why. If they're looking for us, it'll be harder for me to keep the shield up.'

Keller climbed out of the hatchway. 'I'll make every shot count. I promise.'

Ayl followed him, and together they hurried up to the top of the hill where Dray had made her charge.

They looked down to see her standing helmetless at the foot of the hill, surrounded by Nara-Karith, moving like a sleepwalker as she unsheathed her *trunga* knife and held it out. One of the aliens reached up to take it.

Keller fired. The Nara-Karith flew backwards with half its head missing. The others clicked frantically and scrabbled around, trying to see where the attack had come from. Two more shots, and two more aliens fell dead, limbs twitching.

'Keep moving!' Keller urged Ayl. 'We've got to get to her fast!'

With Keller firing, they made their way down the hill to the edge of the battleground. The area was littered with dead aliens, uncollected pieces of armour and discarded weapons still to be picked up. The Bellori soldiers by the command centre stood still, looking just like ordinary people now that their armour was gone. Only Dray still looked anything like a proper Bellori now, in what remained of her armour.

Keller's aim had been as true as he'd promised, Ayl thought. The Nara-Karith seemed to sense that any of their number who got close to Dray would be shot, and were going crazy looking for the sniper.

The rifle clicked. Keller gave Ayl a look that said *out of ammo.*

He threw his rifle away, picked up a Bellori k-gun and kept firing. Ayl stayed close behind him, the dry surface of Bellus gritty beneath his wide bare feet. The Nara-Karith were only twenty paces away now.

They're hunting for us. Ayl could feel the pressure of their minds on his, hammering at his mental wall. He had never faced this many before. He had to keep himself and Keller concealed, but the pressure on his mind was increasing all the time. He felt like thousands of glinting bug eyes were peering into his skull.

'Almost there,' Keller whispered, edging closer. 'Keep that field going, Blue! Once I'm close enough . . .'

Ayl didn't even hear Keller's next words – something about grabbing Dray and running – because they were drowned out by the Nara-Karith, whose thoughts were pounding in his head like sledgehammers, throbs of bright red pain: *SEEK. LOCATE. DESTROY. SEEK. LOCATE. DESTROY.*

He gritted his teeth and redoubled his efforts. The cloaking field was holding, but barely. He felt like he was holding up a collapsing wall with his bare hands.

'I'm not sure how much longer I can keep this up,' he said in a strained whisper.

The inside of Dray's head felt like cushion stuffing.

Once, when she was little, she'd 'borrowed' a hoverbike and gone for a ride down Hellback Canyon. The bike had hit a rock pillar and she'd been thrown from the saddle, breaking her leg in three places. Only her armour had kept her from dying.

Why was she remembering that now? Oh yes – the surgeon had injected her with anaesthetic, and this was how she'd felt back then. She felt vague and dreamy, like she was floating in a huge balloon.

Something was niggling at the back of her mind. There was something she was supposed to do, something very important. *Did I forget?* she thought woozily. *Is my father going to be angry with me?*

She groped around inside her mind, trying to put her finger on it, but it was like trying to catch an eelviper with her hands. The important thing kept squirming away from her. It was no good. She couldn't remember what it was.

She blinked twice, but her eyes didn't seem to be working. *Did I have another accident?*

Her arms and legs felt numb, just like they had when the surgeon had treated her. He'd had to take her armour off to put the splint on her shattered leg, and she'd been so embarrassed she'd cried . . . she could hear the surgeon's voice in her mind now, angrily telling her to take off her armour.

'I won't!' she mumbled. 'You can't make me . . . I won't.'

The voice was louder now, more insistent. It didn't even sound like the surgeon any more. *Take off your armour.* It was cold, rasping, alien.

'Not . . . taking . . . armour . . . off!'

Someone's worried face was staring at hers. It was a friendly face. She was sure she'd seen the young man somewhere before. What was his name? Weller or Yeller or something.

TAKE OFF YOUR ARMOUR, roared the voice from somewhere in her head. *DISOBEDIENCE WILL BE PUNISHED.*

Suddenly a lean blue-skinned youth was staring at her too. *That's an Aquanth*, she thought dreamily. *We learned about them in military school. They're pacifists. The instructor says that pacifist is another word for coward.*

The blue boy was reaching out his hand to her. Maybe she should take off her armour after all. She began to unfasten her breastplate. She wasn't in any danger from an Aquanth, surely—

Ayl's mind touched hers. *Dray, wake up!*

Suddenly, everything was clear. She remembered who she was, where she was and what she was doing. The Nara-Karith were all around her, pincers upraised, but she could feel the power of Ayl's mind blocking their commands out of her thoughts.

They almost had me, she realized. *I was going to take my armour off!* She hastily refastened her breastplate, her heart pounding.

She heard Ayl groan. 'I can't hold it – the cloaking field's collapsing!'

'We need to get out of here,' Keller said beside her. 'Scouting mission's over. Come on!'

Dray could move again now. The numbness was leaving her arms and legs. She turned to answer him – and a vast shadow fell over them, looming like a giant above the Nara-Karith.

Ayl let out a terrible cry and fell to his hands and knees beside her. The Nara-Karith surrounding her gave a triumphant hiss, and she knew Ayl's field was gone. He and Keller were as visible as she was.

She lunged for her k-gun, but the voice that came from the shadow made her stop in her tracks. It was a deep, rasping voice, full of bitterness and hatred. It was a voice she *knew*.

'Well, well, well,' it growled, taking a rattling stride towards her. 'Can this really be the famous General Dray, cowering at my feet? She thought she was invincible. And now look at her.'

It was a Bellori warrior, but unlike any Dray had ever seen before. Taller and broader than even the strongest soldier in her army, he was wearing overlapping armour plates that encased him completely like some dragonish beast. Her gaze moved up his body to the torso, looking for the tiniest chink in the armour to drive a blade through – and there the nightmare began.

The massive arms that emerged from the shoulders were human enough, but the four extra limbs that extended from the shoulders and flanks were those of an enormous Nara-Karith. Dray couldn't tell if they were grafted on to the armour, or – and she prayed it wasn't so – if they sprouted from the flesh of the living person inside it.

All the arms, human and insectile alike, held different weapons. One held a k-gun, another a vibroblade, another a whizzing rotary saw . . . and they were all trained on her.

She was moments away from dying in six different ways at once.

'Sudor,' she breathed. 'What have you done to yourself?'

8

The last time Keller had seen Sudor, the huge Bellori had been escaping on a stolen ship from a moon called Zarix. His army had been defeated. How could he be back now, and with such an enormous force?

'Your swordfighting is better than your military tactics, *General* Dray,' Sudor mocked. 'Believe it or not, I expected invading Bellus would be a challenge. I spent many turns preparing for this invasion.' He held up his hands in mock surprise. 'But what do I find? The famous Bellori army is nowhere to be found, aside from a few soldiers who don't want to fight!'

'You are ankle-deep in your own dead,' Dray snarled.

'I expected worse losses. And I believe I have you to thank for leaving Bellus so vulnerable. It was your decision, yes?'

Don't answer him, Keller thought despairingly. But Dray's silence was all the answer Sudor needed.

'I thought as much. You have made this invasion easy for me, General Dray. I have snatched your planet as easily as plucking a ripe samthorn fruit.'

'You haven't taken Bellus yet!' Dray spat back at him. 'We'll fight you.'

'You already tried, and you already lost,' Sudor sneered. 'The entire Nara-Karith race is here, and they hunger. Hundreds of thousands stand ready to plunder your world. How will you stand against them, with your pathetic defence forces?'

'So you found more eggs after all, did you?' Keller interrupted. 'Isn't that lucky? Saves you from having to do any fighting yourself!'

'Remind me to cut out that clever tongue of yours,' Sudor growled. 'Oh, I did better than just *finding* more eggs. I unravelled the secrets of their DNA and made more into my cloning vats. These Nara-Karith warriors are the first to be hatched in a laboratory, nourished by my very own cells. And best of all, this new mutation can self-replicate – so my creations will live on forever!'

'So you're the bugs' queen now?' Keller said acidly.

'They are my creations. My children!'

Keller stared at Sudor's extra limbs. 'Yeah, I can see the family resemblance.'

Sudor laughed. 'Ah, yes. These. Versatile, aren't they?' He extended and retracted the limbs, like a grotesque claw opening and closing. 'Behold, the new hive-master of the Nara-Karith. Just as my essence passed into them, enhancing their mental powers and rendering them immune from Aquanth manipulation, so theirs has passed into me.'

'Those extra legs – they're *part* of you?' Keller felt sick.

'Oh, yes. I am no longer merely a Bellori. I have remade myself, mutating my body, splicing my genes with theirs.' Sudor shook a gauntleted fist. 'See, boy, a new trinity is born in me – a fusion of the Nara-Karith, my own genes, and the power of science! We are one. One army, one species, one master race!'

Keller heard Ayl's horrified thoughts in his mind: *Three become one! The prophecy. Is that what it meant? Dear Gods of Aquanthis, no. It can't be.*

'You're completely insane, Sudor,' Keller whispered.

Sudor shrugged off the comment. 'Words, Trade King Keller. Just so much hot air. I prefer real weapons. Do you see how my Nara-Karith are gathering up every last Bellori weapon? My mothership will soon be filled with the most sophisticated arsenal in the nine galaxies. The entire Trinity System will fall before me!'

Sudor spread all six of his arms wide, as if he were trying to grasp for the stars. 'Nothing will stand in my path! Every Bellori, Cantorian and Aquanth will be my slave! I have won, do you hear me? I have won!' He threw his head back and let out a maniacal laugh to the heavens.

'I must have damaged his brain when I shot him in the face back on Zarix,' Dray hissed.

'I have a new face now,' Sudor said slowly. 'Do you want to see?'

He reached up to his helmet and twisted it with a sharp crack. Keller badly wanted to look away. Like being trapped in a nightmare, he couldn't take his eyes off Sudor.

Steadily, the helmet was lifted off. Keller's stomach lurched as he saw what was under there. He had expected a mass of scars where Dray's failed assassination had wounded the man, and perhaps an eyepatch, but this was far worse.

Sudor had truly made himself one with the Nara-Karith. One human eye stared out from his demolished face, filled with fury and madness. Bulging from the other eye socket, bloated and huge, was the green multifaceted eye of an insect, surrounded by wiry hairs. The stub of a half-grown antenna, twitching feebly, protruded from the forehead above. Something hooked and pale bulged from the corner of Sudor's mouth. With horror, Keller realized it was a half-grown mandible.

'We'll never submit to you,' he said, defiant despite his nausea. 'None of the three worlds will!'

Sudor chuckled, a low thick sound like bubbling oil. 'Is that a fact? I think you've already seen that my many-legged friends can force you to do whatever I desire you to do.'

He gestured behind him, to where the column of Nara-Karith snaked all the way back to the ship. They snapped their claws and gnashed their mandibles impatiently.

Ayl's head was still aching from the effort of keeping the cloaking field up. At least he didn't have to focus on it any more now that Sudor had seen them, he thought. He could recover some of his strength, though he doubted he'd be able to use it for anything. There were just too many enemies here, and Sudor's willpower was stronger than his own.

'Once these weapons are loaded up,' Sudor gloated, 'we'll be taking over the Bellori command centre. You know what that means, don't you?'

'You're going to try to take over the whole Bellori fleet!' Dray yelled.

'Oh, I'm going to do a lot more than try. Any ships whose crews do not surrender will be destroyed.'

'That's not possible,' Keller scoffed. 'Those ships are controlled by trained pilots! You can't just shut them down at a distance by flicking a switch!'

Dray's face was ashen.

'Dray?' Ayl asked. 'He can't do that . . . can he?'

'Three words, children,' Sudor said smugly. 'Central. Command. Database.'

'What the heck is that supposed to mean?' Keller yelled.

'It's a centralized security system. It constantly tracks the movements of every ship in the Bellori fleet,' Dray explained reluctantly. 'We implemented it last turn, after *he* turned our own ships against us on Zarix. We couldn't take that risk again!'

'She thought it would stop me stealing any more Bellori ships!' Sudor said, laughing. 'Of course, I'll be using it to intercept any ships the Bellori try to send against me. You'll have no chance of taking me by surprise. You never expected anybody to invade the command centre, did you, Dray?'

Dray raged at him. 'Nobody has ever invaded Bellus! And nobody ever will!'

'And yet I have. A fatal oversight. You seem to be making a lot of them.'

'So have you,' Dray snapped, pulling out a communicator. 'You only have one ship, and it's on the ground. That was *your* fatal mistake.'

'What are you going to do?' Sudor smirked. 'Drop bombs on me?'

'Since you mention it, yes.' Dray activated her com. 'Say goodbye to your army and your ship. My flagship's in orbit with enough bombs on board to scatter your ashes from one end of the Trinity System to the other. We're going to nuke your worthless hide to the other side of the universe!'

Then Sudor did something Ayl could never have expected. He laughed out loud, sounding genuinely amused by the idea.

Keller was right, he thought. *Sudor is completely insane. His experiments on his own body must have pushed him over the edge.*

'Bomb my ship, Dray? Come, now. We both know you're not going to do that,' Sudor said with an evil smile.

Ayl waited for Dray to argue back, but she just

glared sullenly at him. Ayl blinked. This didn't make any sense at all.

'No more games. I'll give you one chance,' Sudor said. 'Instead of watching your people die by the million and your fleet explode ship by ship, you can do the smart thing and surrender. I promise you, I'll be merciful.'

'Merciful?' Dray spat the word out as if it tasted foul.

'The Bellori will be allowed to live as slaves. They will have plenty to do, I assure you. My Nara-Karith are messy creatures, and will need to be cleaned up after. Mines will need to be dug, and new ships built. It will not be a pleasant life for the Bellori, but it will be a *life.*'

'I would rather die than bend a knee to you!' Dray said.

Sudor simply shrugged, his extra limbs flexing. 'Very well. Don't say I didn't offer you the choice. Soon, you will be just one more skull on the pile.'

He leaned down until his disfigured face was millipaces away from Dray's. Ayl kept a close mental hold on her. Suddenly he was sure he knew what Sudor was going to do next.

He's going to mind control her – force her to say she's

surrendering, so all her people can see her do it! It's not enough for him just to win. He has to humiliate Dray, dishonour her in front of her people! All because she beat him in the blood challenge . . .

'You know what choosing war will mean,' Sudor hissed into her face. 'You know what you are throwing away by defying me. You should be ashamed. Your father would certainly be ashamed of you!'

It's all down to me, Ayl thought. *I have to do something NOW.*

He grabbed Keller by the hand and pulled him towards Dray. Keller looked alarmed, but said nothing.

'Do you want to be remembered as the general who destroyed your world?' Sudor roared.

'Better that than being the one who handed it to you on a plate!' Dray screamed back at him.

Now, Ayl thought to himself.

Sudor brought his two lowest arms in close, ready to seize Dray around the waist. She stared up at his hideous face and set her jaw, refusing to scream no matter what agony he might inflict. *If I die this day, I'm going out like a true Bellori*, she thought.

A hand grabbed hers. Ayl. He was holding Keller's hand too. His voice in her mind said *Hold on tight.*

'How sweet,' Sudor mocked. 'Your little friends have come to hold your hand while you die. Don't worry, lads, I haven't forgotten your people. Aquanthis and Cantor are next.'

The claws clamped painfully around Dray's waist. Sudor held up the arm carrying the vibroblade, turning it in the sunlight. The sun glinted off its razor-sharp edge as Dray struggled uselessly in the iron grip. The arms lifted her off the ground. Ayl's hand tightened in hers.

'One quick stab right through the eye and into the brain,' Sudor purred. 'An eye for an eye! How apt.' The blade quivered above him like a scorpion's sting. He bared his teeth in a cruel grin. 'Don't worry. You won't even feel it. Give my regards to your father.'

The blade flew at her face.

Then there was a sudden, overpowering feeling of being pulled, then Dray was – somewhere else. She was falling through a tunnel of swirling energies. The feeling of falling seemed like it would never end, like falling down into a bottomless pit in a nightmare.

Typhoon winds seemed to roar all around and through her. Rocks and sand wheeled above and below her, ghostly transparent. She could see the stars through them. Her own body felt icy cold and empty, as if she had become merged with space itself.

Time seemed to have slowed down to a trickle. A milliclick felt like it was lasting forever.

For a deathly cold moment, she expected to look down and see her impaled body below her. Sudor couldn't have missed, she knew that. She was dead, and the winds were blowing her to the afterlife. If this was dying, it wasn't so bad. There was no pain, and at least she'd see her father again.

But then she began to remember. She'd done this before, or something like it, when she and Keller and Ayl had mentally travelled to Aquanthis. That giddy sensation of rushing through space – that was where she'd felt it before!

Only now it wasn't just her mind that was travelling. It was her whole body.

Ayl, she realized, holding her breath in awe. *He has more power than I ever imagined! He's not just moving objects with his mind any more. He's teleporting us through space!*

9

The moment he felt that strange tugging sensation all over his body, Keller guessed what was going on. It was just like the feeling he got before a ship entered warp, that mysterious, magical state that enabled spacecraft to travel across lightpaces in clicks. It felt a little like the giddiness you get in your stomach just before a lift plummets eighteen floors.

Some people dreaded entering warp – Keller's elderly aunt had always claimed it made her space-sick – but Keller loved it. But this was even better! It was like warping through space with your head out of the window!

He had never felt sensations like this before. They were travelling faster than thought itself, volleying through rocks and earth that were no more solid than mist. Maybe this was what comets would feel like, if they could feel . . . burning through the depths of space in streamers of ghostly fire . . .

Keller's hair stood on end as the world rushed past them, transformed to a silvery-blue whirlwind of shadows. There was his Mazakomi racing ship, up ahead at the end of the tunnel of swirling light. Dray and Ayl, beside him, looked like glimmering outlines of their usual selves.

Ayl had somehow turned the laws of physics upside down and inside out through willpower alone. This journey was only taking a fraction of a click, and yet Keller could savour every moment of it.

We're the first people ever to enter warp without a ship! he thought excitedly.

He grinned as he remembered all the racing ships he'd flown, all the tournaments he'd competed in, looking for the ultimate thrill. The gull-like Vesper, the triple-finned Ryshanko Elite, even the completely transparent Diamond of Shuv that an alien prince had let him borrow for a day. Not one of them compared to this.

With a jolt, he fell into the cockpit of his own racing ship and collapsed gasping on the plush seats. Ayl and Dray landed in a sprawl next to him. For a moment they lay there together, too exhilarated to move or say anything.

Keller turned his head to look at Ayl. 'That was

awesome, Blue!'

Ayl levered himself up from the cushions. 'I wasn't sure I could do that.' He pinched the bridge of his nose and winced. 'I've thought about it, of course, but the energy cost . . .'

Keller started laughing again, still giddy from the jaunt through space. Then he saw the alien spaceship looming over the rocky crags and remembered *why* they'd had to escape. *We all nearly died*, he thought. *Bellus is overrun. And here's me celebrating because I had a wild ride.*

All of a sudden he didn't feel like laughing any more. He strapped himself into the pilot's seat and set about preparing the ship for take-off. Ayl and Dray fastened their own safety harnesses alongside him.

Dray filled a glass of water from the ship's built-in drinks dispenser and passed it to Ayl. 'Thanks, Blue. You saved us.'

'My pleasure,' Ayl said, knocking it back in one.

Dray looked down. 'I've lost count of the number of times you've saved my hide, you know that?'

'Think nothing of it,' Ayl said. He tried to smile, but pain showed on his face. Keller checked the vent intakes and the life support.

'Hey, Keller?' Dray said.

'Hm?' Keller grunted, not looking up. He ignited the engines, ready for a quick take-off in case the Nara-Karith saw the ship and came swarming over it.

'I'm sorry,' Dray said. Her body sagged and her head drooped, as if her armour were suddenly ten times heavier. 'I shouldn't have pulled a knife on you.'

Keller shrugged.

'I just . . . I went crazy for a moment when I saw what they were doing to my world. I knew I had to stop them and I'd cut down anyone who got in my way. I didn't mean to threaten you! You're my friend, my comrade in arms, my . . .' She slowly clenched her fist. 'I swear on my blood oath and on my father's ashes, I'll never do anything like that again.'

Keller had to smile. 'Hey. Don't beat yourself up. It was my fault.'

'*Your* fault?'

'Yeah. I should have known better than to try to come between the Bellori General and her people. Everyone knows that's in the top ten things to do if you're tired of living!'

'Get us out of here, Keller,' Dray said. 'We've still got work to do.'

'Firing her up!' said Keller, punching buttons. 'Where to?'

'Find one of those pods the ship dropped. I need to know what Sudor's other troops are doing here.'

As the Mazakomi lifted away from the surface, Ayl tapped Dray's shoulder and pointed to the screen. 'Look. Your gun cam is still running.'

Dray saw the Nara-Karith were still busily gathering up weapons, loading them on to the spider craft in a continuous circulating column. Her heart sank even further when she saw what the rearmost ones were carrying.

'Those are elite guard rifles,' she said, pointing. 'Only the Bellori who guard the command centre carry those. The Nara-Karith must be inside already.'

We stood unconquered for thousands of turns. Now Bellus is falling in less than an hour. How could all of this have happened so fast?

The Nara-Karith carrying her gun was marching towards the command bunker now. Hundreds more Nara-Karith were swarming in through the main doors, while up above on the fortified battlements, Bellori soldiers stood passively watching them. Dray wanted to scream at them to fight, but now she knew what they were going through. If it hadn't been for Ayl's rescue, she'd be standing like that herself right now.

'All the armour in the world wouldn't help them now,' she said. 'Guns, missiles, plasma blasts, you can ward them all off. But mind control? It's unfair. There's no honour in it!'

'That gift should never be used as a weapon,' Ayl nodded.

'You've used it as one,' Dray reminded him sharply. 'Against the Nara-Karith.'

'Only when we were fighting for our lives on Zarix,' said Ayl.

'Any which way,' Keller said, 'we're alive now. Sudor's not won yet, Dray.'

'Look at the screen!' Dray pointed. 'Does it look like we've got a hope? I *failed*, Keller!'

'Don't blame yourself,' Keller tried to say, but Dray let out a howl of fist-pounding grief that drowned out his words.

'This *is* my fault,' she said miserably. 'I gave the orders. I thought moving troops off Bellus would be a better defence.' She gave a sour, humourless laugh. 'I might as well have told my people to go and repaint their houses in their own blood. All my life I wanted to lead. I never thought that leading might not mean winning.'

'Dray, listen!' Keller said. 'This looks bad. I won't deny it. But it isn't over. Sudor wants you to think it is, but it's not.'

Dray fought back tears. 'What do you mean?'

Keller reached over and laid his hand on her armoured shoulder. For a moment she imagined the warmth of it through her thick armour plate.

'You've saved thousands of lives here today,' Keller said gently. 'Think about it. If you hadn't moved those troops off Bellus, they'd be here now, wouldn't they?'

Dray nodded.

'And they would be under Sudor's control now, just like all the rest!' Keller jabbed a thumb at the viewscreen. 'But they're not, because those troops were out there across the Trinity System, on your ships, manning your stations and sentry posts, far away from Sudor and his army of bugs. Think about what that means.'

Dray tried, but all she could think about was how scattered and useless her army had been, unable to stop Sudor's ship from heading straight to Bellus. What had Brancur called it? *A paper shield.*

'Every one of those soldiers is on his way back to defend Bellus!' Keller finished. 'You couldn't be in a better position to take Sudor on if you tried! Don't you see? You haven't wasted your army, you've *saved* it!'

He was right. Dray's brain instantly went into overdrive. All the forces from the outlying stations, all the deep patrols, all the squadrons guarding the trade routes and the waypoints . . . they were all heading to Bellus, on her orders. They were all outside Sudor's control. And they would be looking to her for leadership.

Pull yourself together, she told herself.

She pushed Keller's hand off her shoulder as if she were brushing off a fallen leaf, and sat up straight in her chair. 'The leader of the Bellori people doesn't give up without a fight,' she said, feeling fresh energy pounding through her veins. 'If you thought otherwise, you were badly mistaken!'

Keller grinned. 'Glad to hear it, General.'

'Guys?' Ayl said, pointing out of the cockpit window. 'I see one of the pods.'

The ovoid pod had come down in the desert, far from any of the Bellori bases. All around it, gaping pits had been dug into the planet's surface. Nara-Karith were vanishing into them and coming up with their pincers full of minerals, tipping them on to huge heaps that lay nearby. It was ugly, a brutal mutilation.

'I can hear their thoughts,' Ayl said. 'They're saying "Gather ores, gather ores."'

'They're strip-mining Bellus?' said Keller, sounding horrified.

No. Please, please not that. Dray felt a new fear seize her, more terrible than anything else that had happened today. *Sudor, you maniac, you're endangering our whole homeworld!*

'Those pods fell all over the planet. We have to stop him,' she said desperately. 'He's insane. There has to be a way!'

'I might not be the professional warrior here,' Keller said, 'but I kind of like the idea of just nuking that kracking mutant maniac off the face of the planet, along with all these plundering bugs of his.' He shrugged. 'Subtle it's not, but hey, it would be effective. And the explosions would be pretty.'

Dray was silent.

'Dray?' Keller said. 'Your flagship is loaded with fusion bombs, right? So do it! Give the order and blow them all to smithereens! What are you waiting for?'

'I wish it were that simple,' Dray sighed. 'OK, you two. Listen and don't interrupt. There's something you both need to know.'

* * *

Ayl could sense the unease radiating from Dray. *She's getting ready to tell us something big. Something secret.* His own palms felt damp and achey in sympathy, as if it was *him* who was nervous.

'Bellus,' Dray said slowly, 'has an unstable core.'

'Uh,' said Keller, 'when you say unstable, you mean . . .'

'I told you not to interrupt!'

'Sorry.'

'Imagine a beronzium fusion reactor the size of an entire world. Now imagine it's cranked up way beyond safety limits, *and* the casing is cracked all over, *and* the beronzium inside is constantly on the verge of meltdown. That's Bellus.'

'The casing is cracked?' Ayl said. 'You mean the planet's *crust?*'

'Haven't you noticed what the scenery is like out there? Rivers of magma, exploding volcanoes, boiling lava pits? We get earthquakes all the time, too. When Bellori are young, they're told it's the motherworld roaring to keep all other creatures in the universe away from her children.' Dray sighed. 'When we get older, we find out it's us that have to defend her.'

'But almost all planets have molten cores,' Keller objected. 'Surely Bellus can't be that different?'

'Yes it can,' Dray said darkly. 'The Trinity System isn't like other places. We all know it, but nobody ever talks about it.'

'So that's why you would never let us mine all those rich ores under your planet's surface,' said Keller in wonderment. 'It would endanger your whole world. I thought you were just hoarding them for yourselves!'

Ayl was staring out at the burrowing Nara-Karith, thinking what a vulnerable heart lay under the planet's armour. He thought about Dray's words – *it's us that have to defend her* – and slowly a startling truth began to dawn in his mind.

Everything I've ever believed about the Bellori is wrong, he thought.

'You've known Bellus was unstable for a long time, haven't you?' he asked Dray.

'For as long as the Bellori people have been warriors,' Dray said. 'Which is another way of saying "forever".'

That proved it.

'Oh my celestial fountains,' Ayl said, shaking his head in awe. 'This changes everything.'

'I don't get it,' Keller frowned.

'Open your eyes, Keller! All this time, the Bellori have let us go on believing they were warmongers, that they lived to fight. But it's the other way around, isn't it, Dray? *You fight to live!*'

'It was a choice we had to make,' Dray said, sounding like she was speaking from the other end of a long tunnel into darkness. 'Our scientists proved that any serious attack on Bellus could set off a chain reaction that would . . .' She paused, leaving the words unsaid. 'We could never let that happen. Bellus had to be defended.'

'So you became the system's greatest warriors,' Ayl said.

'There was no other way. If we had not been the strongest, some other race might have dared to attack us.'

Ayl wondered what the other Aquanths back home would have thought of those astonishing words. *All Bellori are warmongers, it's in their nature*, they had said. *They love to spill other people's blood. It's in their genes.*

All that was wrong. The Bellori had been forced to become warriors out of need, not because they were born to it. They encased themselves in armour and lived and breathed war as soon as they could stand upright. So much sacrificed, all to defend a fragile world.

'That rules out the bombing run idea, then,' said Keller. 'I'm sorry, Dray. I didn't know.'

She shrugged. 'No matter. How could you have known? It's the biggest secret our people have.'

'If we can't destroy the troops,' said Ayl, 'then we need to take Sudor down. Without him giving the orders, the Nara-Karith army will fall apart.'

'Good plan. But getting to Sudor won't be easy,' Keller warned.

'Beating the Nara-Karith was never easy before, either,' Ayl said forcefully. 'But we did it, didn't we? And we can do it again!'

10

The Bellori flagship still hung in space above Bellus like a sword waiting to fall, but it was no longer alone. Answering Dray's urgent call, the Bellori fleet had returned from the length and breadth of the Trinity System. A host of spacecraft now surrounded the *Astyanax* like hovering arrowheads.

Dray stood on the bridge, giving her report to the Security Council while behind her the planet Bellus loomed on the viewscreen. Grim and silent, her generals waited for their chance to speak. When Dray explained how the Nara-Karith had used mind control, an explosion of angry voices broke the silence and she had to quieten them again.

'Sudor will have taken the command bunker by now,' she said, 'and plundered all the weapons in the local arsenals. His troops are scattered across the planet, digging under the surface and strip-mining our minerals and ores. We don't have to guess what he's planning next. He hasn't tried to hide his plans, he's even boasted of them to us. He means to conquer Cantor and Aquanthis and enslave us all.'

'You speak as if Bellus were already his!' roared Brancur.

'Bellus has fallen,' Dray said sharply, and her tone made Brancur fall silent. 'We are no longer fighting to defend her. We must fight to win her back.'

'Then send the fleet in to bombard Sudor's forces!' Scraa said, thumping a bulkhead as he spoke, as if he were pounding nails into a coffin.

'We cannot use fusion bombs and you know it,' Dray shot back at him.

'Then use fire, or poison gas! A true warrior knows many ways to kill.'

'None of which work on the Nara-Karith,' Vayne pointed out in his hoarse voice, and once again Dray silently thanked the black-armoured general for his words. '*Gas*, General Scraa? Against a foe that can withstand the vacuum of space?'

Scraa folded his arms. 'So how do you suggest we destroy the armies currently infesting our home?'

'A surgical strike on Sudor, as General Dray herself suggests,' Vayne hissed. 'To destroy the nest, you must target the queen.'

'You *hope* that will work!' sneered Mursh. 'Where is your proof?'

'Study the records as I have done, fool!' Vayne roared in sudden anger. 'General Dray killed the hive queen at the battle of the asteroid, where the Nara-Karith were first defeated! It turned the tide of battle!'

'Enough discussion,' Dray said firmly. 'We have our plan. Sudor must be neutralized using stealth. General Vayne . . .' She took a deep breath. 'I need the services of the Shadowfire Elite.'

'As you command.' General Vayne's voice showed not a trace of emotion.

Dray had lived her life in awe of the Shadowfire Elite, the secret team of commandos who lived to serve the Bellori commander-in-chief. They did not officially exist, and were only ever used to carry out the most deadly operations deep inside enemy territory. Stealth was their watchword, and their training and equipment made them ruthlessly efficient.

Other worlds knew of them and feared them. Keller had joked about them in her hearing once: 'On Cantor they say that if the Shadowfire Elite cut your head off with a whisperknife, you won't even know about it until you sneeze and your head falls off.'

Only Cantorians would dare to joke about these people, Dray thought as the Shadowfire Elite assembled in front of her on the bridge several moments later. *The Bellori know better.* There were ten of them. Their armour was charcoal-grey, but Dray knew it could mimic any background. Too bad they'd be leaving it behind this time . . .

'We're going to sneak into the Bellori high command bunker and launch a surprise attack on Sudor,' Dray told them. 'To do that, we'll have to pretend to be under the Nara-Karith's control. And that means removing our armour.'

She began to remove hers, and the Shadowfire Elite followed suit without a word of complaint. Soon they were standing together in their one-piece combat overalls, looking just like the hapless enslaved Bellori down on the planet's surface.

Keller had been fidgeting nervously while they undressed. 'You can't go in without weapons!' he protested eventually. 'It's suicide!'

'Who said anything about going without weapons?' replied Dray.

She held her arm up in front of Keller and pressed a tiny button on her wrist. A foot-long blade made from translucent red material, the width of two fingers and thin as a single hair, sprang from the end of her sleeve.

Keller stared. 'What kind of a knife *is* that?'

'The sort that makes people afraid to sneeze in case their heads fall off,' Dray told him. She sharpened the edge against a microbrasion grindstone until it looked sharp enough to cut a hair in two lengthways. A second press, and it whipped out of sight, making no noise.

'Shadowfire Elite, equip yourselves,' Dray ordered. 'Micro-ordnance and stealth weapons only.'

Along with her wrist-mounted whisperknife, Dray selected two full clips of nano-grenades from the armoury, fastening them around her ankles. Each tiny sphere, despite being no larger than a samthorn seed, could blow a ten-pace crater in the dirt. The Shadowfire Elite donned grenade clips of their own, along with some of the most secret weapons in the entire Bellori arsenal: monofibre whips, coiled filaments that looked like spiderweb but were as strong as diamonds; derma pockets, patches of fake skin that concealed wafer-thin, razor-edged throwing discs; and even fingerdarts, microscopic needles laden with venom that nestled under the fingernails and could be loosed with a flick of the wrist.

'You surely can't be thinking of going *with* them?

Let the Shadowfire Elite do their job,' General Scraa said soberly. 'What if the operation fails?'

'We'll need a backup team on standby to pull our fat out of the fire,' Dray said, ignoring General Scraa's reservations. 'Assign the Eighth Blood Legion to the job.' The Eighth Blood Legion were, in many ways, the direct opposite of the Shadowfire Elite. Armoured as heavily as tanks and equipped with artillery that could blast entire buildings to rubble in a matter of clicks, they were not stealthy – but they could dish out a lot of damage.

Dray hesitated before speaking again. 'Keller? I need to ask you for another favour. There are risks involved. Significant risks.' *Of all the Cantorians I could ask to risk his life for the Bellori*, she thought, *why does it have to be the trade king himself?*

'Just ask,' Keller said.

'I need you on the strike team. Sudor's bound to have messed with the data systems inside the command bunker. And you can hack computers like nobody else I know.'

'Better find me some overalls, then,' Keller said. 'I wouldn't want to stand out.'

Dray turned to Ayl. 'I'm sorry. I have to ask something of you, too.'

'Of course you do,' Ayl said with a calm smile. 'You need me to join the strike team. I'm the only one here who can protect the team from the Nara-Karith mind control. Though I won't be able to control *them*, I'm afraid. Sudor designed this new breed to be immune to anyone's influence but his.'

'You understand there will be a lot of killing?' Dray said.

'You can't fight destiny,' Ayl said, and the look in his piercing eyes left her feeling as if someone had walked over her grave.

We'll see about that, Blue.

'Tactical computer?' Dray called. 'Give me a holo-map of the terrain in sector Alpha Prime subsector JD-436.'

A ghostly image of the Bellori command bunker, overshadowed by the huge alien spacecraft, appeared on the bridge. Dray, Keller, Ayl and the Shadowfire Elite members gathered around it, the light from the projector bathing them in red.

'Listen up,' said Dray. 'This is the plan . . .'

What would my mother think of me now? Ayl thought. *Dressed in combat overalls, about to go on a kill or capture mission with an elite team of Bellori operatives?*

Not the future she would have wished for her son, I guess . . .

The elevator doors opened on to Hangar Bay 88, where signs read TOP SECURITY and COMMAND PERSONNEL ONLY. There was only one ship in the entire hangar, a small, sleek craft with wide flat wings like a manta ray. It was so black that light seemed to be sucked into it.

Keller gave a low whistle. 'Now that's a cool ship. I bet she's fast!'

'She is,' Dray said. 'Fast and virtually silent.'

'Does she have a name?'

'Not yet,' Dray said. 'So far she's only flown on test flights. You'll be the first pilot to fly her in a combat situation. We've been calling her Prototype Omega.'

'Catchy,' Keller replied with a smile.

With ten Bellori soldiers crammed in alongside Ayl, it was uncomfortable inside the stealth ship. Ayl hoped it would be a short flight.

Keller fired up the engines and the ship took off in ghostly silence, rocketing down the launch tube and into space.

Ayl prepared the team for telepathic communication. He reached out with his mind, sharing his thoughts with Dray, Keller and the Shadowfire Elite, linking their minds together.

This is a mind-share, he told them. *It's how we're going to block the Nara-Karith out. It may seem strange at first, but you'll get used to—*

Instantly the Bellori soldiers rebelled. *Get out of my head!* he heard one of them thinking. *How dare you intrude!* Another was so outraged he thought, *Back off or I'll kill you, Aquanth!*

They all struggled to break free of the mind-share, with an anger that took Ayl by surprise. To him, a mind-share was like diving into a warm sea and breathing in the clean water. Why did they hate it so much? Then he understood. They had already taken off their armour. Now they believed they were exposing their innermost warrior souls – their most private thoughts. They couldn't stand to be laid bare like this.

It's OK, he quickly reassured them. *I won't invade your privacy. Just focus on the job at hand.*

He drew on the energy of their anger, transforming it, channelling it into strength to shield them. *You fight as a group. Your strength comes from your unity. Think of this mind-share as an extension of that. Together your minds have a better chance of repelling any enemy assault.*

* * *

'Landing in five,' Keller called out loud. 'Everyone buckle up.'

The Omega Prototype touched down silently as a cat's footfall. They had come down in the main courtyard of a Bellori fortress set into the side of a mountain, which looked like it had been in use for thousands of turns. Pulson turrets now stood on top of the ancient stone walls, but they were silent and unmoving. Metal walkways led around the interior, littered with empty rifle racks and opened ammo cases. No soldiers were here now, living or dead.

The team climbed out of the hatch and stood surveying the scene.

'We've missed the fighting,' Ayl said, feeling a little relieved.

'He's right,' said Cavalya, the captain of the Shadowfire Elite. She was dark-skinned and shaven-headed, with the lean build of a professional hunter. 'The bugs have been here already. No weapons left to take.'

'We're not here for weapons, Captain,' Dray told her. She pulled on some strange-looking goggles with thick indigo lenses.

'X-ray goggles!' Keller said, impressed. Ayl heard

129

what he was thinking: *I've got some of those back at home, but they weren't for military use.* He shook his head. Keller was a good friend, but he acted like a schoolboy sometimes.

'Over here!' Dray said, running to the back of the fortress. She dug her fingers into the dirt at the base of the rear wall and pulled up a hidden trapdoor. An iron ladder led down into the tunnel below. A dim, muddy amber glow came from beneath.

'Nice work,' Ayl said as the team climbed down. 'How did you know this was here?'

'Being commander-in-chief gives you access to a lot of interesting old files,' Dray said. 'I learned about an abandoned tunnel system under this part of Bellus. It was meant to move troops around the planet at super-fast speeds, to coordinate emergency city defence.' She crooked one corner of her mouth in a half-smile. 'But then the Cantorians sold us a new fleet of airborne troop transports, so the tunnels fell into disuse.'

'At least the lights still work!' Ayl said.

'Only just,' Keller complained. The old striplight above his head was flickering, and barely gave enough light to see by as it was.

'If the lights are working, the podcar rail transports

should be too,' Dray said. 'Come on. This tunnel leads straight to the high command bunker.'

Shortly after, as they hummed through the near darkness in a musty podcar, Ayl felt the first shadowy filaments of Nara-Karith thoughts brushing against his mind. He shuddered. They were getting closer . . .

Keller wished he was back at the controls of the Omega Prototype instead of being wedged into this ancient, obsolete Bellori vehicle. The air was barely breathable and the podcar screeched as it went around corners, like a rusty old carnival ride. *I suppose I should be grateful it still moves at all.*

They suddenly slowed down, almost throwing Keller out of his chair as the vehicle lurched and then ground to a halt.

'There's the entrance up ahead,' Dray said. 'And look at this.' She shone her torch on to a rounded surface of dark metal that had smashed clean through the walls of the tunnel and into the earth below. 'If that thing had come down a few paces to the left . . .'

'What is it?' Captain Cavalya asked her.

'We're looking at one of the ship's legs,' Keller said. 'It dug itself deep into the surface of Bellus. Must have smashed right through this tunnel.'

Captain Cavalya looked at the riveted metal surface with disgust. 'He defiles us. I wish to kill him myself. With my bare hands.'

Dray had reached the reinforced blast doors that led into the command centre. A dusty security console stood off to one side, with a white cursor blinking on the screen. It was a very old-fashioned model, not the sort of thing anyone would invest money in nowadays. Keller wondered how long it had blinked like that into the gloom.

Dray tapped in her password. 'Get ready to act brainwashed, everyone!' she ordered. 'Anything could be waiting for us on the other side. Bugs, our own people, even Sudor himself. We have to keep up the pretence until it's time to attack. Ayl, keep up that mind screen. OK. Go!'

The Shadowfire Elite let their shoulders sag and their heads droop. Dray hit the ENTER key.

A rude buzz sounded. ACCESS DENIED, read the message on the screen.

'Oh, damn you, Sudor!' Dray shrieked in frustration. 'He's locked me out! Keller—'

Keller was already running over. 'Step aside, General.'

He took out his handy *Hackmaster Pro*, a flat silver

gadget the size and shape of a dataslate, and connected it up to the terminal's power wires with a couple of clips. A few keystrokes later, a medley of random characters blitzed the screen, flickering through millions of combinations until the correct code was found. A soft *ding* came from the console, and the doors slid open with a clattery wheeze.

'You might want to beef up your security,' Keller told Dray with a grin.

Beyond the doors was an empty hangar where vehicles would once have been stored. Other doors led off in all directions. The sound of heavy crates being dragged came from behind a set of doors at the far end.

'This is it,' Dray whispered. 'Everyone act like you're under their control. Let your faces go slack and move slowly.'

Just try to keep your minds empty, echoed Ayl's voice in Keller's head – and the heads of the strike team, too, by the look of them. *You're going to see things that will make you angry, maybe even afraid. You may see people you used to know, people you want to help. Remember, there's nothing you can do right now. Just stay calm, listen to my voice, and tune the bugs out.*

Moving in a slow shuffle like zombies, the strike

team filed through the doors and into the room. It had been an arsenal, but now the shelves and storage lockers were being emptied. Subdued Bellori soldiers, stripped of their armour, were passing crates full of ammunition and weapons to Nara-Karith, who carried them out of the room's far exit.

Gather arms, gather arms, went the signal in Keller's mind like a pounding headache. He shook his head and concentrated on the mind-share, tuning out the chanting.

None of the enslaved Bellori even looked at them. The Nara-Karith looked up as they entered the room. For a moment, their antennae quivered and Keller saw Dray reach for the button on her wrist. Then the Nara-Karith went back to loading weapons, and Dray led the team across the room and out of the far door.

They moved quickly through the bunker's hexagonal plascrete corridors, following signs for the data chamber, until the door was ahead of them. There were two Nara-Karith guarding it, but no Bellori in sight.

Dray glanced once at Captain Cavalya, who nodded. A flick of the wrist, and the air shimmered for an instant. The top half of the leftmost Nara-Karith slid off the bottom half.

Monofibre whip, Keller thought. As the other sentry turned stupidly to see what had happened, another Shadowfire Elite member pointed at it, and a tiny flash came from his fingertip. The Nara-Karith swelled like a balloon, jiggled its legs helplessly and burst. *And that would be an explosive fingerdart!*

Dray jerked her head. 'Inside, fast.'

Inside the data chamber walls of computer equipment loomed on all sides, outlined with thin red neon strips. Now this, Keller thought, was state-of-the-art technology. From this hub, the entire Bellori fleet coordinated their operations.

'Take a look, Keller. Tell me how bad it is. Everyone else, guard the entrances.'

Keller found an access terminal. Keys rattled as he checked the network, scanning the whole system as fast as he could to get an overview. It was bad, all right.

'He's got access to the entire network, like you thought,' Keller said. 'And he's running a live link back to his ship. I think he's trying to download the whole Bellori intelligence archive!'

'Can you stop him?' Dray demanded.

Keller flicked through screens for a few clicks. Then a slow smile spread across his face. 'Oh, I can do better than that. This is amateur work. Sudor's forgotten one critical fact!'

'Tell me!'

'His ship is connected to this datacentre – but the connection runs both ways. We can access his ship's systems from here!' Keller typed furiously, accessing the craft's governing computer before the security protocols noticed what he was doing. 'Crazy. It looks like his systems are made from recycled parts . . . OK. I'm in. Let's start by killing that ship's engine so it'll never fly again.'

He rerouted some systems so that the ship would permanently confuse its waste disposal subroutines with its propulsion system. *That should make for an interesting flight. Short and smelly . . .*

'He's bound to notice you've been messing with his systems,' Captain Cavalya warned.

'No he won't,' Keller assured her, keys rattling under his fingertips. 'I've built a false front. This will all look like normal activity. Oh, and I've scrambled the data feeds from the hub, too. He'll think he's able to take over the controls of any Bellori ship – but he'll be wrong.' Keller cracked his fingers. 'And to think that my father used to tell me I was wasting my time playing holo-games . . .'

'Someone's coming!' called one of the soldiers. 'We need to get out of here!'

'Just a few clicks more,' Keller insisted. 'Come on, where are you . . . ?'

He scrolled through digital maps of the command centre, hunting for one special signal. Reflected screenfuls of information flashed in his eyes.

Then he turned to face Dray and her team.

'Found him. He's in the high command chamber.'

11

I didn't need a computer to tell me that, Ayl thought to himself. He could feel Sudor's presence close by, a powerful, malevolent aura that ached in his brain like a rotten tooth. He could only wonder how a Bellori had become such a master of telepathy, when it was supposed to be the Aquanths who were Trinity's psychic adepts.

The feel of Sudor's mind, even at a distance, made his skin crawl. It had been bad enough when the demented tyrant was human, but now the Nara-Karith DNA had changed him to something against nature itself, a horror that had no place in the universe.

So much power, and reeking of evil. Ayl felt like a tiny creature in the shadow of an immense baneshark, too small to be noticed at first, but not for long. *He's going to sense my presence soon, just like I'm sensing his. Then he'll come for me.*

Ayl redoubled his efforts. He drew deep on his

strength, remembering his long hours of training on Aquanthis, strengthening the mental wall that blocked Sudor's thoughts out from his own.

The team was moving again now, trudging down endless corridors where enslaved Bellori laboured and Nara-Karith struggled to haul weapons up to the surface. The bunker was all plain plascrete, with rivet-peppered metal doors and exposed pipes and wires running across walls and ceilings. Bellori had about as much time for interior design as they did for religion.

Ayl quickly learned that the Nara-Karith didn't even have to concentrate to control the Bellori around them. Their dominating mind-waves were always present, like the hypnotic scent of a flesh-eating plant.

As they were passing a Nara-Karith sentry, Ayl noticed that Captain Cavalya's eyes were glazing over far too convincingly. He quickly cleared her clouded mind, strengthening the shield around them all as best he could.

'Two more levels,' Dray whispered. 'Stay focused, everyone.'

Ayl groaned. Every time they passed a Nara-Karith, the Bellori's minds would begin to fog over like a pool turning to ice and he would have to strain to bring them to their senses. Groups of Nara-Karith were even worse.

The strain of defending the whole team was wearing Ayl down. *I've taken on far too much*, he realized, *but it's too late to back out now.*

Every beat of his heart drummed fresh agony into his brain. Sweat poured from his brow and he could feel the veins on his neck pulsing painfully. He thought of asking the Shadowfire Elite medic for a shot of painkillers, but that might numb his mental powers, too. He'd have to tough it out, even if it felt like *trunga* knives were being slowly pressed into his skull.

By the time they reached the uppermost level, Ayl wanted to cry out loud. The Nara-Karith were standing guard in almost every corridor. Keeping the team's minds free was like carrying shards of red-hot iron. He thought he could taste blood, but wasn't sure if the sensations were his own or belonged to one of the Bellori.

Ayl was dimly aware of a huge security door in front of him, guarded by two massive Nara-Karith holding looted Bellori weapons. But it was what lay behind the door that made him clutch his forehead and squeeze tears of scalding pain from his eyes. Sudor was in there. He could feel the man's power roaring in his mind like the volcanoes of Bellus itself.

My head's going to explode, Ayl thought. And in that moment he honestly believed it would. Maybe Sudor was telekinetic, too. Maybe Ayl's head really would burst from within. The pressure was becoming too much to bear . . .

Dray glanced to her left and right. The Shadowfire Elite stood ready, still pretending to be under the Nara-Karith's control. She had ordered them not to intervene, except on her command.

The two bugs who guarded the door made a suspicious chittering noise. *HOLD STILL FOR INSPECTION*, they suddenly broadcast telepathically.

'Inspect *this*!' said Dray, flicking her whisperknife out and thrusting it up to the hilt in the bug's face.

Before the other one could react, half of the Shadowfire Elite let fly with razordiscs, severing limbs and leaving the alien flailing helplessly on the floor.

'Nano-grenades out!' she ordered, moving clear of the door. Dray did the same. The remaining team members primed nano-grenades and threw them at the door in a single well-practised movement. The explosions were deafening, the crash of the door landing inside the room even louder.

The command chamber was full of smoke from the nano-grenades, but Dray could see Sudor's huge helmeted form already beginning to move, rising from his chair and turning around. *Got you like a scrath-rat in a trap, you scum*, she thought.

Dray began to run as the world went into slow motion. Her whisperknife was already out and ready, thirsting for traitor's blood. Sudor's arms were moving too – he was going for a gun.

Dray flashed back to when he had loomed over her before. Between his helmet and his neck armour was a tiny crevice, almost impossible to see. As he brought his gun up, she thrust the whisperknife at that hairline crack and forced it in deep.

A terrible howl came from inside the helmet, turning into a rattling gurgle.

Like a tyrant's statue pulled down by an angry mob, Sudor toppled over backwards. The ground shook beneath Dray's feet as he hit the ground and lay unmoving.

Dray held her breath. She stood motionless, watching Sudor's immobile form for any sign of life. There was none.

I need to see his face, she thought. *I need to make sure he's truly dead this time.*

Slowly, cautiously, she knelt down beside him. She gripped his helmet with both hands.

But before she could yank the helmet off, a limb lashed out and sent Dray spinning back across the room. Sudor reared up. With one hand he clutched at his throat, where blood was seeping between the armour plates. His other arms were reaching for weapons.

'Did you really think it would be that easy?' he croaked, his voice rasping with blood.

Dray flipped up on to her feet in a single acrobatic move and shifted into a combat-ready stance. 'Roaches are hard to kill, too,' she snarled.

With that, she attacked.

She jabbed, sliced and thrust, her blade grating against his armour. She ducked back out of his reach as the long limbs whipped out, then circled him warily, waiting for the next chance to strike. He backed up against his command console, on the defensive now, holding his limbs up in a wary guarding stance.

Dray didn't turn around, but she could sense Keller and the rest of the team hanging back, ready to attack but reluctant to fire in case they hit her. Good. It was only right that the honour of the kill should go to her, the Bellori commander.

She drove her blade, still wet with Sudor's blood, hard at his stomach. You could split the armour plates with a hard enough blow. He knocked her thrust aside, then blocked the follow-up smash she aimed at his head. She fell back again, panting, then lashed out in a blinding flurry of slashes, punches and kicks.

Not one of them connected. Sudor had six arms, and the advantage was more than she could contend with. Every sweep of her blade, every bone-crushing kick or punch, was parried by an insectile arm.

Sudor's counterattacks were heavy and slow, but there were so many of them, she soon tired. Every hand or claw held a different weapon. She had to dodge k-gun shots, parry vibroknife blows, duck the power saw that whizzed past.

Slowly, Sudor drove her back. He lashed out with limb after limb, while Dray tried to find a target to strike at and fought to avoid being pinned up against the wall.

'Don't ever start a fight you can't win, Dray,' Sudor gloated.

A scythe-like blade shot at her face. She barely parried it in time before another arm struck at her from her blind side, knocking her off her feet with the force of a power hammer. She slammed into the wall, then fell to the concrete floor.

He'd cut her – no way to tell how deep. Searing pain flooded up her side. If her whisperknife hadn't been strapped to her arm, she would have dropped it. Never had she longed for her keratin-plated armour more.

Dray clambered back to her feet more slowly now, breathing hard and wincing as the wound in her side stretched. Sudor advanced on her swiftly. Dray weakly tried to parry the double-jointed limb that swept towards her, but a stout pincer clamped around her throat. Locked tight, she was lifted struggling into the air. She hacked at the pincer desperately, but another arm seized her wrist, twisting it aside.

Sudor lifted the arm that held the vibroknife up to Dray's throat.

'How do you like that, General?' he spat.

'Open fire!' Keller yelled. 'Take him down, *now*!' He knew they might hit Dray – but she'd be dead in seconds anyway if they didn't act!

Fingerdarts and razordiscs peppered Sudor's armour. He turned with a roar, holding Dray like a swaying puppet.

Keller remembered that the dead Nara-Karith at

the door had been carrying Bellori rifles. He grabbed one and loosed off three rounds at Sudor, knocking him off balance.

As Dray struggled in the hangman's noose of Sudor's grip, Captain Cavalya flung a razordisc. It sheared through the arm that held Dray, severing it. She fell to the ground, clutching her throat and gasping for breath.

Sudor bellowed in frustration and turned to attack the Shadowfire Elite. They returned fire with all the weapons they had. A monofibre whip slashed the end off another of his arms and razordiscs studded his armour from head to foot, but nothing could slow Sudor down. A vicious bash from one arm sent Captain Cavalya flying through the air and slamming hard into a wall.

A door at the far end of the room hissed open, and a platoon of Nara-Karith burst in. They clutched freshly looted Bellori weapons. Sudor gave a grunt of satisfaction as they lined up behind him. Keller's heart sank. Those weapons would tear the unarmoured Shadowfire Elite to shreds in seconds.

Ayl screamed in pain, as if something was giving way inside his skull.

Retreat! came Dray's voice over the mental link they

146

still shared. She was on her feet, running back the way they had come. *We can't win this! There's too many of them! Fall back and rendezvous with the Eighth Blood Legion!*

The members of the Shadowfire Elite just stared blankly at her.

'Retreat! That's an ORDER!' Dray screamed – this time out loud.

Now Dray's own Bellori team were pointing their weapons at her. Dray stared, unable to understand what had happened.

A horrible feeling came over Keller as he realized he could no longer feel the Bellori linked to him mentally. Ayl's network had all but gone. Now he could only feel himself, Dray and Ayl still connected.

We've lost them, he thought, looking at the blank faces of the Bellori assassins.

This was not just defeat. This was something even worse. The Shadowfire Elite, the most feared strike team in the whole system and beyond, had fallen under the control of the Nara-Karith.

12

The nearest assassin's face showed no emotion as he raised his monofibre whip. Dray was horrified to find herself trapped between Sudor and the Nara-Karith on the one side, and her own brainwashed soldiers on the other.

What the krack do we do now? Keller's voice rang in her mind.

We run, Dray thought back.

She lowered her head and charged, aiming for the gap between two soldiers.

The assassin's whip flashed out, missing her by a whisker, scything through a ceiling pipe that released hissing steam into the room. Dray broke through, shoving soldiers out of the way, running back the way they had come.

She glanced over her shoulder and saw Keller hauling Ayl by the arm, while the Shadowfire Elite moved like zombies to pursue them. *Thank the Fates the mind control slows them down. If they were fighting at their full potential, we'd be dead.*

'Running away again, Dray?' Sudor's mocking voice boomed down the corridor. 'Too much of a coward to stand and fight?'

The words stung her like venom, but she kept running. One day she would spill his blood, she promised herself. One day she would savour the sweet taste of revenge. *But not today.*

'Back to the tunnel,' she yelled back to the others.

They rounded a corner. Nara-Karith guards moved to block their way, aiming at them with stolen Bellori weapons. With a savage snarl, Dray went into a forward roll, came up between them and spun on the spot, whipping her whisperknife around in a lethal circle to decapitate both of the aliens at once. As she wiped her knife clean, Keller blasted at a third bug behind them who had come to help the others.

Crimson lights began to flash from the ceiling. Alarm klaxons blared a constant rising and falling howl.

'So much for stealth,' Keller said. 'Sudor's sounded the alarm. Every bug in this place is going to come down on us now!'

'The Eighth Blood Legion will be here soon,' Dray said. 'Come on!'

At least it's an honest fight now, she thought grimly. *I'd hated sneaking around like a thief in my own command bunker.* She caught Ayl's eye, and what she saw made her fear for his life. He was gasping for breath and his eyes were bloodshot. *Keeping us protected from their mind control is killing him! We have to get out of here. Too bad he can't cloak us in a stealth field, too . . .*

The tunnel entrance was on the other side of the weapons storage room. It was still full of Nara-Karith and enslaved Bellori. The soldiers didn't even look at Dray, but the bugs hissed in alarm and went for their weapons.

'Get them!' Dray yelled. She and Keller fired and fired again, shattering the bug-like aliens to pulp before they could get a shot off. One huge Nara-Karith flung a heavy ammo crate in Dray's direction, but she dodged it easily and her next shot blew the creature to bits.

Once the bugs were dead, Dray half hoped the Bellori would come to their senses and fight on her side, but they were still unpacking boxes with slack, expressionless faces. The mind control must be coming from the whole Nara-Karith army at once, she realized. They couldn't hope to free her people unless they wiped out every single one – or Sudor himself.

They burst through the doors into the hangar. There was the tunnel entrance ahead of them – with about thirty Nara-Karith, armed with Bellori weapons, between them and it. And the tunnel doors were *closing*.

The Nara-Karith opened fire with their k-guns. Dray dived behind a pile of crates just as Keller pulled Ayl down behind a support pillar. *Ayl's nose is bleeding. We're losing him. And if he goes, we all go.*

Dray and Keller broke cover for long enough to shoot one bug each, diving back just in time as the bugs returned fire.

'What do we do?' Keller panted. 'Stand and fight?'

'Not against that many,' Dray said. Part of Keller's pillar blew off as a k-gun shot slammed into it, sending rattling shrapnel flying. Then she heard a desolate clang as the tunnel doors shut, cutting off the tunnel completely. 'So much for the podcar. Going to have to find another way out.'

'Lead on!' Keller yelled. 'I'll cover you!'

Keller roared a battle cry as he raked the Nara-Karith with gunfire. Dray dashed back through the door they had come through. The deafening racket of rifle blasts suddenly stopped as Keller's ammunition gave out. He threw the rifle at the oncoming bugs and ran after her, with Ayl stumbling along behind him.

Dray led them back through the labyrinth, making for the bunker's main entrance. She killed without even slowing down, using her whisperknife to slash at any Nara-Karith unfortunate enough to get in her way.

Just a few more clicks, she told herself. They were almost out of the bunker now. Ayl could barely walk and Keller was bleeding from a cut to the head, but they were alive. She punched a door control.

There, at last, was the bunker's main entrance, thick with Nara-Karith guards. It was just as crammed with bugs as the tunnel had been, but Dray saw the blast door had only just begun to descend, while a siren hooted its warning. There was still hope.

'Oh Gods, there's too many!' Keller groaned. Ayl's breath wheezed painfully behind them.

Dray unhooked the loop of nano-grenades from her ankle, activated one and flung the whole lot at once. The Nara-Karith made a skittering, hissing noise, levelled their weapons at her – and then a white-hot flare erupted in the midst of them, milliclicks before the staccato bangs of multiple explosions.

'Let's go! Move!' She ran for the smoke-filled door and dived under it. Keller staggered through, coughing, pulling Ayl behind him.

Dray yelled into her wrist-com. 'Requesting backup! We need immediate evac!' Where *were* they? 'Eighth Blood Legion, come in!'

The bunker door ground shut behind her. The smoke from the nano-grenades was starting to clear now. Dray peered through it, hunting for any sign of her backup squad.

Ayl was sagging against Keller now, looking more dead than alive.

Keller stood braced, wishing he'd had the chance to grab a weapon. The Eighth Blood Legion had better be out there to pick them up. He could still fight, with his bare hands if he had to, but he was no Bellori and he was exhausted.

He felt a surge of elation as he saw a row of Bellori k-guns emerge from the smoke. *They made it!*

But then the smoke cleared completely and his joy was swallowed up in despair. Those weapons were in the hands of Nara-Karith, standing fifteen abreast. They moved to surround the bunker entrance in a semicircle. Among them were Bellori soldiers, stripped of their armour and clearly under the bugs' mental control.

He glanced at the door controls. No time to hack them, with the enemy closing in. And even if he could, they'd just be trapped inside the bunker.

'We can't go forward and we can't go back!' he said to Dray, who crouched beside him in a combat stance.

'Backup squad, *come in*!' Dray screeched into her com.

'Ayl?' Keller said desperately. 'We need you.'

'I . . . can't . . . nothing   left . . . dizzy . . .' Ayl clutched his head, his eyes struggling to focus as he swayed dangerously from side to side.

Keller resisted the impulse to shake him by the shoulders. 'Can you teleport us out of here?'

The Nara-Karith took aim. There was a sound of dozens of safety catches being released at the same time.

Ayl blinked his reddened eyes. 'I'm sorry . . .'

Keller and Dray exchanged a glance. Suddenly Keller wanted to say something, but the words jammed in his throat and wouldn't come out.

From up above came a sudden roar of jets, growing louder as something descended towards them. Keller looked up and saw the gunmetal underbelly of a Bellori heavy assault ship, the access hatch wide open. Ropes came tumbling down towards them.

'Start climbing!' Dray ordered. She fanned out a set of razordiscs and sent them zipping through the packed horde of bugs, each disc claiming a Nara Karith life.

Keller caught hold of a rope and pulled himself up, gripping with his knees as he went. His mind flashed back to the forest near the Royal Palace on Cantor, and the rope swing he'd played on as a child. *That was the last time I climbed a rope . . .*

A bright flash shot past his face. That was a plasma rifle round, he thought dumbly, and climbed even harder. The rescue ship still seemed kilopaces above him. The air lit up with plasma rounds, peppering the space around him like fireworks. He held on for dear life.

There was Dray, scrambling up her rope like she was born to it. Even Ayl had hold of one now. Rifles boomed angrily beneath Keller and waves of heat washed over his arms and legs as plasma orbs missed him by a whisker.

'Winch us in!' he screamed up to the Bellori in the ship above, dangling by one arm. 'We're holding on! Just winch us—'

The ship began to lift, bearing them high above the ground. *Finally!* Then something smashed into his left arm like a white-hot bar of iron.

I'm hit! His upper arm exploded with agony as if the bone had shattered into burning bits. He lost his grip on the rope and suddenly slipped, clutching at air, falling. Far below, the ground loomed up to receive him.

'Keller!' screamed Dray.

She swung, kicking out with one leg. Keller grabbed for it and connected. The hard impact of her boot in his stomach kicked the wind out of him. But he clung on with one arm, gripping the rough fabric of her combat overalls. Dray reached down and grabbed a fistful of clothes as the Eighth Blood Legion winched them slowly on board.

It was all Ayl could do to cling on to the rope without blacking out. He was dimly aware that the ship above was getting closer. Next thing he knew, a heavily armoured Bellori was holding out a hand to him, helping him on board.

'Up you get, Aquanth. We've got you. Come on.'

'Battle's no place for one of *his* sort,' commented another of the soldiers. 'The boy's a mess.'

'Don't let the general hear you say that,' Ayl's helper warned. 'Way I hear it, this one's different. She

156

trusts him and that's good enough for you and me.'

Ayl didn't even care. He lay on the ship's floor, the cold metal against his cheek. Steadily the howling winds died down as the hatch was closed and locked, leaving only a distant roaring in his ears. His face and head were a mass of pain, as if they had been battered with clubs. *At least we're alive*, he thought. *But the Bellori soldiers we went in with . . .*

The shield hadn't been strong enough. He'd given everything he had and it hadn't been enough to save them. Now they were Sudor's slaves.

'Hold still,' said the Bellori soldier who'd spoken up for him. He was unscrewing the lid from a large plastic bottle. Next moment, Ayl felt cool water splashing over his face, running down his neck, moistening his parched gills. The searing pain in his head slowly began to ease.

'There's more in the locker if you need it,' the soldier said, setting the bottle down beside him.

'Thanks,' said Ayl.

He could smell burned cloth and singed flesh. Across from him, Keller was wrapping a bandage around his blackened upper arm. He sucked air through his teeth at the pain.

Dray was sitting silently on a metal bench, lost in

her own thoughts. She looked small and vulnerable, stripped of her bulky armour. As Ayl watched, wondering what to say, she screwed her face up in despair and hit herself hard in the forehead with a balled fist. Keller glanced over. Dray hit herself again and again, viciously.

'Hey,' Keller said, grabbing her wrist gently but firmly. 'Hey. That won't make anything better.'

Dray tugged, but he held on. Eventually she gave in and let her arm go limp, tears rolling down her cheeks.

'That was our one chance,' she said, sounding dead inside. 'I blew it. I failed.'

'You can't blame yourself,' Keller said softly.

'It doesn't make any difference if I do or if I don't. He's won.'

Ayl came and sat beside Dray, the pain in his head beginning to fade. 'Which is more important? The planet Bellus, or the people who live on it?'

'The people, of course!' she spat. 'You really think I want to hear philosophy at a time like this?'

'Hear me out,' Ayl persisted. 'Your people must survive, right? Well, back where I come from, the fish that survive when the banesharks come aren't the ones who hang around and wait. Those fish get eaten. The survivors swim away as fast as they can, whole schools of them.'

'My people aren't fish,' Dray said wearily.

'But they are in danger. And if you want your people to survive, they need to get the heck away from here. Do you understand what I'm saying?'

Dray stared at him in disbelief. 'Evacuate? The entire *planet*?'

'Yes,' Ayl said, gently wiping a bloody tear from her face and leaving a dark smear like warpaint. 'It's the people you're sworn to protect, not the rocks and sand they live on. Get your people out of the way, then you can bomb Sudor and his Nara-Karith to kingdom come without endangering any of them.'

'How can I get them away when they're under the bugs' control?'

'My people could help,' Ayl said. 'If all the Aquanths worked together, we could shield the Bellori, just like I shielded you. We couldn't keep it up for long enough to fight a whole war, but we could give them the chance to retreat.'

'Even if that worked, we don't have the ships . . .' Dray protested, but Ayl could tell she was thinking it through.

'You do have the ships!' Keller put in. 'The entire

Bellori fleet is gathered here, on your orders! And that's just the warships. You've got cargo haulers too, and all the commercial ships Cantor has berthed at their ports.'

Dray opened and closed her fist. 'Evacuate the planet, then bomb Sudor. It could work . . . No, it's impossible. If we attacked, we could trigger a chain reaction! Bellus itself could be destroyed! And if that happened, with the three worlds so close to one another, Cantor and Aquanthis could be destroyed too!'

'Then we'll just have to evacuate Cantor and Aquanthis as well,' Keller said softly. 'Right, Ayl?'

'Right,' Ayl said. 'It's the only way.'

'You don't know what you're asking!' Dray pleaded. 'I've already lost so many battles . . . now I might destroy my own *homeworld*!'

'Bellus may not survive,' Ayl said. 'And even worse may come if Bellus is destroyed. But that's a sacrifice we might have to make, Dray. Sudor has to be stopped. There's no other way to save your people . . . and ours.'

13

Dray stood on the command deck watching her generals file into the room. She'd been tended to by the Bellori medics and put her armour back on. Her mouth was dry and her heart pounding. She wished she were anywhere but here, any other time than now. If only she could turn back time, make her father alive again . . .

They don't know what I'm going to say. None of them even suspect.

'All present,' said Scraa as the last of them entered. 'Shall we begin?'

Dray nodded. For a moment, nobody spoke.

'General, we are anxious to know what you propose to do next,' said General Mursh.

Dray swallowed. 'As you are aware, Sudor . . . is alive. The mission was a failure, though we did disable his control over our fleet.' The dreaded words fell rapidly from her lips. If she paused now she might never speak again. 'All members of the Shadowfire Elite are under Nara-Karith mind control. The entire planet is infested by Nara-Karith, who are stripping our planet of its ores, causing irreparable damage. There is only one course of action left to us. We must immediately evacuate Bellus, Cantor and Aquanthis. Once the population of each planet has been safely evacuated, we can begin to . . . to . . .' She coughed nervously. 'To *bomb* Sudor's ship and the command centre. If we can kill him, we cripple his army once and for all.'

Ten terrible clicks of silence passed. Dray was shaking inside her armour.

'For shame,' said General Scraa, very slowly. 'For *shame.* The ancestors look on us this day, General Dray, and they turn their faces away as they see what we have become. Is defeat not enough? Must you add dishonour as well?'

'Scraa speaks for all of us,' said Brancur. 'You know such an attack is wrong, and yet you hide behind outsiders, knowing we cannot speak of the reasons why in their presence!' He glanced at Ayl and Keller. 'This council of war is a travesty.'

'They know,' Dray said.

Brancur roared like a wild beast and slammed both

162

his fists down on the table. 'You *told* them? Our greatest secret, shared with outsiders?'

'Is nothing inviolable to you, Dray daughter of Iccus?' spat deep-voiced General Corm.

'My people!' Dray snarled back at him.

'A fine way you have of showing it!'

'General,' implored Mursh, 'let reason prevail. We cannot sanction a bombing run on Bellus. I will put it plainly: Bellus might be destroyed.' He folded his arms. 'That cannot be allowed to happen.'

Dray stood up. She pointed at the huge viewscreen that hung before them. 'You all wish to talk about inviolable things, about things that cannot be allowed to happen? Take a good long look, all of you.'

On the screen, unarmed and armourless Bellori were meekly doing as the Nara-Karith told them. They shuffled back and forth lifting boxes and dragging crates.

'What is a planet, compared to the freedom of the people who live there?' she demanded. 'Look at our people! Look at what Sudor has done to them!'

All the generals looked at the slack-jawed faces, the glazed eyes. Captain Cavalya stumbled into the picture, shoved brutally by a huge Nara-Karith. She bent and scraped up some loose pieces of armour from the floor.

The bug shoved her again, knocking her to her knees.

'Do you see? If *this* is our future – if this is the only Bellus we have left – then I say it isn't worth saving! There's one thing more important than our home. Our freedom.'

The generals mulled it over.

Scraa eventually spoke up: 'If we were to go ahead with this attack, and Bellus was destroyed – what then? Where would our people live?'

Keller stood up. 'The Bellori will always be welcome on Cantor,' he said. 'I know you don't think much of us merchants, but we never forget a valued customer. Or a trusted friend.'

'Thank you for your offer of hospitality, Trade King Keller,' Dray said with an icy calmness she did not feel. 'Cantor proves itself a worthy ally, as always. But the Bellori cannot depend upon the charity of others. If worst comes to worst, then we will take to the stars. We have military outposts across the Trinity System with more than enough room to house the entire Bellori population.'

'Whole families, growing up on outposts?' said Mursh uncertainly.

Brancur snorted. 'I grew up on an outpost. Made me the man I am.'

'It will be hard,' Dray said, 'but we are a hard people. One way or another, we will survive. And one day, we will claim a new homeworld.'

'Then let it be decided!' Scraa urged.

'Very well,' Dray agreed. 'The council will now vote. I propose that we evacuate Bellus, Cantor and Aquanthis and commence a full-scale attack on Sudor's forces. All in favour, raise your fists.'

Scraa raised his fist. Then Mursh, then Brancur. One by one, the generals all raised their fists. Only General Vayne was left, a dark figure sat apart from the others.

Vayne. He was a hero to his men, Dray remembered. Again and again he had defended Bellus against her enemies. If he refused the attack, then she was lost. It could mean rebellion, civil war . . .

'We may lose our planet,' Vayne said at last. Then, taking a deep breath, he added: 'But we must never lose our liberty.'

He raised his black-armoured fist.

'Patching you through to the Cantorian Trade Council now, Your Majesty,' the helmsman told Keller.

The images of Yall and Tyrus appeared on the holoscreen, towering above the Bellori on the bridge.

Behind them, in a solemn-faced row, stood the other Trade Council members. When they saw Keller standing there, their expressions of wariness changed to scowls of rage.

'Gentlemen,' Keller said. 'We need to address a grave matter of planet-wide importance. We must—'

'Do you have any idea how worried we've been?' Tyrus roared at him. His flared, hairy nostrils gaped on the screen, revolting in their magnified hugeness. 'What were you thinking, taking off to Aquanthis on your own?'

'We are esteemed councillors, not babysitters to be given the slip!' Yall raged. 'You have managed to endanger yourself and insult us all in one move!'

'Some among us hoped that your coronation might bring a new maturity,' huffed Tyrus. 'Fool that I was, I assured them it would! "He'll settle down now," I told them! "Now he's got a trade king's responsibilities, he'll turn over a new leaf." You made a liar of me, boy!'

Yall narrowed his eyes. 'Is that a bandage on your arm? It is, isn't it? What tomfoolery have you been getting yourself into now?'

'Both of you will hold your tongues *at once*,' Keller said, and there was steel in his voice. 'This is your only warning. Speak to your trade king without the proper respect again, and I will dispatch both of you to the Galactic Rim to supervise an asteroid mining operation for the rest of your lives. Do you understand?'

'But I—' blustered Tyrus. 'That's preposterous!'

'Do you understand?' Keller repeated, slowly and clearly.

Tyrus's mouth opened and shut like a fish. Behind him, Yall was staring in dumb fury. The other Trade Council members were muttering angrily among themselves. 'He's gone too far this time,' one of them said.

'Your trade king is right to demand respect,' declared Dray, moving to stand in front of Keller. 'He has fought to save your lives today, and shown bravery that any Bellori would be proud of!'

'General Dray,' Tyrus pleaded, 'it is hardly appropriate for a trade king to endanger himself—'

'Were you given permission to speak?' roared Keller. 'The commander-in-chief of the Bellori is *talking*! Interrupt her again, you old bean-counter, and it will be your own teeth you have to count! Do I make myself clear?'

'Yes, sir,' Tyrus said stiffly. 'Sorry, ma'am.'

Dray's voice became low and filled with menace.

'Keller has risked his life to save others, while his Trade Council have been lounging in safety on Cantor counting their wealth. And *you* dare to scold *him*? To accuse him of having done less than his duty? How DARE you insult your own trade king?'

Tyrus and Yall stood stock still, silent as guilty schoolboys.

'Trade King Keller,' Dray said, 'feel free to address your trade councillors. I believe they are ready to listen to you now.' She turned her back on them, muttering, 'If they were *my* advisors, I'd make them fight me in the gladiatorial arena for that.'

Keller did not waste time gloating. *Tyrus is wrong*, he thought. *I'm not the raw youth I used to be. Saving our three planets is much more important than rubbing one old enemy's nose in his own humiliation.*

'We need to evacuate Cantor,' he began. 'What I have to tell you is in the strictest confidence. The planet Bellus is unstable . . .'

As he explained the situation, the looks on the trade councillors' faces steadily changed from shock to disbelief, then fear, and finally dread.

'But surely,' said one of them after he had finished, 'even if – Gods forbid – Bellus were to be destroyed, why would that affect Cantor?'

'The three worlds are in alignment!' Keller said. 'The chance of fragments raining down on Cantor is too high. A meteor shower like that could destroy entire cities.'

'Even so, a full-scale evacuation? Isn't that a little too dramatic?' Yall said smoothly. 'Aren't we forgetting something? If we abandon our planet, even for only a day, we lose trade! Imagine it – every single business on Cantor, forced to shut down!'

'Excellent point,' muttered Tyrus. 'Perhaps the Bellori can find some other strategy. Something less catastrophic.'

'Evacuation would cost a fortune!' called one councillor.

'The losses would run to the billions!' yelled another.

'A whole day's trade,' Keller said darkly. 'Well. That *is* a lot, isn't it? Tell me, how many days would we have to trade to replace every single coin in Cantor's treasury?'

Confused muttering broke out among the Trade Council.

'And how many days of work to replace every single crop in our fields?' Keller went on. 'Every fruit, every grain, every herd beast?'

'Obviously, it would take many centuries,' Yall floundered. 'I don't understand . . .'

'Because that's what the Nara-Karith are coming for. They want all of Cantor's riches. The Bellori can't blast them to bits unless we clear our people off Cantor first. This isn't about a few days of lost trade. We could lose the wealth of our entire planet.'

The councillors coughed and looked askance. 'Well,' Tyrus said gruffly, 'when you put it like *that* . . .'

'Spread the word to every citizen of Cantor,' Keller said. 'Prepare to evacuate. I want every single spaceworthy ship made ready to carry evacuees, whether it's a grain hauler or a luxury star-skiff. That's an order, Councillors. Get moving.'

Two down, one to go, thought Ayl. *Here's where it gets tough.*

He sat cross-legged on the Bellori bridge and prepared to contact his mother telepathically. Dray offered him a private room, but he turned her down. Even though the others wouldn't be able to hear what was being said, he wanted them there.

Ayl? His mother's voice was full of worry. *There is terrible psychic turbulence coming from Bellus! A great host of devouring minds, led by an avatar of evil. Get away from there at once, do you hear me? The danger . . .*

Mother, let me speak! Ayl sent urgently. *I have seen it up close, and yes, there is danger. We haven't much time. I'm sending you my memories so you'll understand.*

As Ayl remembered the last hour, he felt her cringe and recoil from the gruesome violence. Every wound, every death by blade or bullet or grenade, made her flinch as if she had felt it herself.

He felt guilty putting his own mother through this horror show, but forced himself to carry on. She needed to know. All of Aquanthis needed to know.

He could feel her weeping when he had finished. *And so, my son, you say we must evacuate? Has it come to this?*

The Cantorians and the Bellori are evacuating, he said.

But perhaps we need not, his mother replied, almost pleading. *Think, Ayl! We can activate the great cloak and hide our world away! That has always been the Aquanth way, to retreat when others wage war, and return when the fighting is done!*

Mother, the time to look at the past has been and gone. The great cloak cannot save us from this threat, nor can it stop rocks a hundred kilopaces across from crashing into our world. You have seen what I have seen: you know that the only way to survive is by standing alongside our brothers and sisters from Cantor and Bellus.

Lady Moa was silent for a long time before responding. When she did, her thoughts were heavy with the sadness as if she carried the weight of an entire race. *You are right, my son. I wished to blind others to our presence. But I find I have only blinded myself to danger.*

Then you'll evacuate? Ayl asked.

I shall call the conclave, came the solemn reply.

Of course. Aquanthis was a pure democracy. No decision as huge as this could be taken without *everyone* being consulted.

Ayl waited as she sent out the mental call to assemble, wondering how he could ever convince his whole people to abandon their home. One by one, the minds of the Aquanths joined together, forming a single telepathic network encompassing the entire planet.

We are gathered. We are One, spoke the voice of the conclave. *What must be decided?*

The evacuation of Aquanthis, his mother told them.

Ayl braced himself for the storm of panic – and it came. Like a tidal wave, the surge of fear crashed across the collective consciousness, mingled with currents of confusion and denial.

His mother stood firm among the uproar, calling for peace until the shouts of outrage had died down to a low murmur. At last there was an expectant silence.

Speak, she finally said. *The people will hear you.*

Ayl was suddenly the focus of millions of minds. He told himself to stay calm. This was no time to get stage fright.

He showed them everything, as he had done with his mother moments before. They saw the gigantic spaceship, Sudor and the Nara-Karith. He showed them the enslaved Bellori, and how Dray was willing to risk the destruction of her home for a chance of saving her people.

There is a prophecy in the great library, he finished, *older than any other writing in this whole system. 'Three become one.' I believe it is time for the prophecy to be fulfilled. The three planets of Trinity must act together as one. We must evacuate, and follow the Cantorians and the Bellori into space.*

Many minds instantly agreed with him, but Ayl heard thousands of voices protesting. *Space is not our home! We belong in the water!*

If true Aquanths understand anything better than the

other races, it's the power of destiny, he replied. *It is time for a leap of faith.*

Now the chorus of agreement was louder. But there were still dissenters. *The Bellori's war is nothing to do with us*, someone was shouting. *Their own violence has led them to this fate. Why should we share it with them? We don't deserve it!*

Ayl held fast. *Many Bellori died to protect us on Zarix. Our fates are already intertwined, for better or worse. Trust to our destiny!*

As the conclave debated, Ayl was reminded of the orchestra at the remembrance ceremony, and how they had tuned up. At first there was only discord, but gradually a swell of harmonious sound began to emerge. They were reaching a verdict.

Waves of resolve converged on Ayl. A decision was approaching, a great and momentous moment in Aquanth history that could never be undone.

The planet spoke with one voice: *Aquanthis will evacuate!*

14

'CORE MONITOR STATION ONLINE,' boomed a robotic voice. 'BELLUS CORE ACTIVITY NORMAL.'

The main screen showed readouts of temperatures, radiation levels and seismic tremors. Dray had patched it through to the flagship so they could tell how Bellus was holding up under the bombardment once it began.

'Almost ready to go,' Dray told Keller and Ayl. 'I've split the fleet into three. The main group to tackle evacuating Bellus, the others to help with Aquanthis and Cantor.'

Keller imagined the sky over Cantor filling with Bellori ships. 'I hope Tyrus and Yall got the word out in time,' he joked. 'Half the planet probably thinks there's an invasion underway.'

'Please. Like we'd choose to live on Cantor!' Dray said gruffly. 'I'll settle for taking my own world back, thanks.'

'We'll help, count on it,' Ayl said. 'You're sure you can take Sudor down?'

'Trust me, he's toast. I've primed the flagship's entire arsenal of fusion bombs – that should take care of his ship – and a whole wing of Firehawks is coming with us to follow up with astron charges. It's time for a little pest control.'

'Well then,' said Keller in a mock-sorrowful voice, 'I guess it's time we bid each other a fond farewell. Unless, of course—'

'No, Keller,' Dray said. 'Don't tell me. I can guess.'

'You can?'

'You're one hell of a pilot, just about the best I've ever known. But I can't keep you here to fly the flagship.'

'Fine,' Keller said with a grin. 'I just wanted to give you the best chance of making it back alive.'

'I think your people need you more than I do right now, don't you? Get them off Cantor and on to the ships. That goes for you too, Blue. Get back to Aquanthis.'

'She's right,' said Ayl. 'We should leave. We'll be with you in spirit, Dray.'

Keller moved to stand beside her. Ayl joined him. They all looked out to the spectacular sight of the sunrise breaking over the edge of Bellus, turning the world into a diamond ring edged with red-gold fire.

'Thank you both for everything you've done,' Dray said. 'For my people, and for me. We'll always be in your debt.'

It hurt Keller's heart to see Dray's home look so beautiful. Strange how different the harsh surface looked from up here.

'I know what I want to say,' Dray said. 'But I can't find the words.'

'CORE ACTIVITY NORMAL,' tolled the electronic voice of the monitoring station.

'We might never see each other again,' Dray said eventually. 'In case any of us doesn't make it, I want you to know you are the best comrades – and friends – that I have ever had.'

Keller laughed. 'You're not going *soft* on us, are you, Dray? That's not like you!'

Dray growled. 'Why, you . . .'

'We'll meet again, all right.' Keller forced himself to smirk. 'And when we do, remember one thing. You owe us for this, Dray. Big time!'

Dray roared, but it was with laughter, not rage. 'I can always count on you, can't I?' Suddenly, she threw an armoured arm over his shoulders, and they were locked in an embrace.

Keller held out an arm to Ayl, who came and joined them. They stood that way for a while, with the Bellori bridge crew bustling around them as if they weren't there.

Three become one, Keller thought.

And then they had to part again.

As Keller headed back to his racing ship, he hoped Dray hadn't felt his heart pounding with fear through her armour. He was more terrified than he had ever been in his life.

By the time Ayl arrived back on Aquanthis, the seas were already churning with people gathering up their few possessions and preparing for departure. A huge group of them swam to the surface, poking their heads up to see the Bellori shuttle touch down.

It was uncanny to see so many eyes silently staring at him from the water. *Sometimes my own people seem alien to me*, Ayl thought. With a wave of thanks to the pilot, he dived into the ocean and swam for the dim shape of Unity Temple nearby.

Persuading the Aquanths to evacuate had only been half the battle. *I told Dray we'd help. My people had better not let me down.*

His mother met him inside the temple, along with around twenty members of the Aquanth priesthood. 'A *second* conclave?' the Naptarch demanded the moment he appeared. 'We are already preparing to leave our beloved planet. What more can you ask of us?'

'Let him speak,' his mother cautioned.

'I've spoken to the Bellori leader,' Ayl said. 'She had a very important favour to ask of us.'

'We do not do favours for the warmongering Bellori,' said a slender-nosed Aquanth priestess who had been one of Ayl's teachers when he was younger. 'They want a war? Then let the blood be on their hands, not ours.'

'Even when we're being asked to save lives?' Ayl retorted.

'Explain,' the Naptarch said.

'Many of the Bellori are still trapped on Bellus,' said Ayl. 'The Nara-Karith have enslaved them using mind control. Sudor's using them as a human shield. He knows Dray can't attack him and risk blowing up Bellus while they remain there.'

'Do the Bellori even care if they kill a few of their own?' another Aquanth elder said archly. 'Why doesn't

General Dray just bomb the lot, and sing sad songs about the valiant dead afterwards?'

'If we refuse to help,' Ayl told her, looking right into her eyes, 'then that's exactly what she'll have to do. Who will have blood on their hands then?'

The elder stared open-mouthed, then looked down.

'There's only one way to do this,' Ayl said. *Seize the moment, they're listening.* 'You won't like it, and I'm sorry, but we have no choice. We have to mind-share with the Bellori, so we can shield them from the Nara-Karith's mind control.'

Disgust flooded the room like a foul stench.

Ayl had once tried to explain to Keller what mind-sharing with another species really meant, and why it was such a taboo to the Aquanths. No comparison he could come up with really conveyed the full horror and revulsion. *Like an alien squirming in your brain,* was the best he could manage.

'It is one thing to mind-share with a predatory beast, to placate it,' said the Naptarch, looking pale and sick. 'Beasts cannot choose their nature. But with the Bellori? You might as well ask us to become cannibals!'

'We can't afford to be squeamish when lives are at stake,' Ayl told him. 'It will not be easy, I know. But you know what would be worse? Watching other people die without lifting a finger to help.'

He looked around and saw reluctance on their faces.

'I thought we were better than this!' he said. 'It's a simple choice. Help our neighbours, or watch them die. If you cannot see the right choice, then you are truly blind.' He turned to leave.

'Ayl!' His mother caught his arm. 'Wait. We need you.'

Lead the chant, her voice whispered in his mind. *Let's show the others the way, you and me. Lead and they will follow.*

The chant began. At first it was only Ayl and his mother, but then, one by one, the other Aquanths joined in. The chant filled the temple, then spread beyond it, with Aquanths in the city taking up the chant and lending their mental power. Hundreds of minds became thousands, then as other towns gradually joined the expanding host, thousands became millions.

Now.

A beam of telepathic power lanced out from Aquanthis to Bellus. As it spread in an invisible halo to embrace the whole planet, the minds of individual

181

Aquanths moved with it, swimming like tiny fingerlings in a tidal wave.

They sought out the minds of the Bellori and merged with them, strengthening them, blocking out the Nara-Karith commands.

In that instant, Ayl felt the Bellori awaken and look around in shock at what had become of their planet. As Ayl explained to them what had happened, the full truth dawned upon the Bellori. They were unarmoured – and unarmed.

Ayl quickly sent a com to Dray and Keller: *It's time!*

Dray clenched the rail below the viewscreen, feeling like a hunter waiting to spring. Suddenly her wrist-com beeped and Ayl's message appeared. She saw her people begin to stir. *Blue did it!*

She yelled up to the communications officer, 'Put me through to the Bellus public address system! All channels!' She would need to choose her words very carefully, as Sudor would hear her announcement as well. She'd had to let him think they were running away, fleeing Bellus like cowards.

'Yes, General. Broadcasting . . . *now*.'

'People of Bellus, this is your leader, General Dray. Our Aquanth allies are shielding you against the

Nara-Karith mind control. However, this is not – I repeat *not* – so that we can mount an attack! Bellus is dangerously unstable and we don't have much time. I therefore order you to evacuate Bellus immediately according to action plan three-seven-nine. All Bellori, make a fighting retreat to the nearest ship for transportation.'

An urgent com from Captain Cavalya flashed on to the screen. 'General, can you hear us?' the captain yelled desperately. 'Our armour has been taken!'

Dray knew every Bellori on the planet was thinking the same thing right now, and she felt a surge of pity for them. 'I repeat, action plan three-seven-nine has been commenced. You are ordered to make your way to the nearest rendezvous point!'

'Our armour's on Sudor's ship!' said one of the Bellori on the screen. 'They took it all!'

'General Dray,' Cavalya said, her voice shaking. 'On behalf of all Bellori who have suffered this ultimate dishonour, I request permission to delay evacuation and retrieve our armour.'

'Request denied,' said Dray. *And it breaks my heart.*

'You cannot deny us this!' Cavalya screamed, and the angry shouts of other Bellori could be heard in the distance. They were grabbing weapons, preparing to attack the alien craft.

'I will not risk your lives. Evacuate immediately!'

'Honour matters more than life!' Cavalya roared. 'We are not cowards! We will NOT abandon our armour and flee!'

'Listen to me,' Dray commanded, her voice booming with authority she didn't know she possessed. 'Your strength does not come from your armour. It never has. It's not your armour that protects the weak, or that chooses to be brave in the face of danger. Your armour doesn't have a code of honour. It's you. Everything that ever made Bellus great comes from *you*, my warrior people.'

Suddenly Dray knew what she must do. In full view of all the others, Dray removed her helmet. The generals on the bridge and the Bellori down on the planet all gasped.

'My father always said that no true Bellori leader should ever ask her people to do something she wouldn't do herself.' Dray removed her gauntlets, unbuckled her breastplate, stepped out of her greaves. 'What you endure, I will endure. That goes for all of us.'

She turned around to face her council. 'Generals! All of you, take off your armour. Show our comrades on Bellus that we stand together as one.'

A grim, dark mood hung over the bridge. Nobody moved at first. Then, slowly, the senior warriors began to remove their armour.

Dray had never seen their faces before. General Corm had streaks of silver in her hair. General Mursh looked so young, not much older than Dray. The warriors glanced at one another nervously.

Dray desperately wanted to reassure them. *It'll be all right if we go through this together*, she thought – but she knew it might not. It might never be all right ever again.

Then came the harshest shock of all for Dray, as a gleaming black helmet was lifted off.

Under his armour, the legendary warrior General Vayne was nothing but a watery-eyed old man. And fear was written all over his face.

15

So big it took up multiple landing zones, the immense Bellori battle cruiser dwarfed the Cantorian cargo runners and luxury planet-hoppers in its shadow. Flying towards it, Keller was grateful for the help – many Cantorians had no ships of their own, and wouldn't be able to evacuate without the help of the Bellori fleet – but he still wished the Bellori hadn't chosen to land it in Cantor's main spaceport. Surely they could have picked a spot outside the city boundaries? Somewhere less congested?

He brought his racing craft down, preparing to dock. Even from this high up he could clearly see the crowds of people churning around the boarding ramps. This was a spaceport, so why weren't they staying in the marked-out lanes?

'Brilliant,' he muttered. 'I'm away from my world for a single day and public order goes completely to hell.'

A section of the battleship's upper hull hissed open to allow his ship inside. Keller parked the racer among a row of frightening-looking interceptors and bombers, each one decorated with images of raptaurs and banesharks. 'What's the fastest way to the main boarding ramp?' he asked the Bellori on duty.

'Elevator down to deck seventeen, Your Majesty.' As Keller turned to leave, the guard stopped him. 'We are evacuating Cantor. I don't have the authority to order you to stay on board, sir, but I strongly urge you not to leave the ship.'

'I'm not leaving,' Keller said. 'I need to talk to my people. Get out of my way.'

The chaos down at the main boarding ramp made a Bellori infantry charge look like an Aquanth meditation circle. Hundreds of Cantorians were trying to cram themselves into the ship all at once, and a row of Trade Council guards had linked arms forming a human wall to keep them back. Some Bellori were watching uneasily, obviously reluctant to step in.

Keller stared in amazement as he saw what his people had brought with them. They were laden down with goods, carrying them on their backs and hefting bulging cases. Many had even brought hover-trolleys so overloaded with possessions they were practically scraping the ground.

The Cantorian guard captain had a voice amplifier, and was making a futile attempt to keep everyone under control. 'Stay in line, please,' his voice blared over their heads. 'One passenger at a time.' He might as well have been chanting nursery rhymes for all the difference it was making.

Keller's eyes narrowed as he saw hands in the crowd waving fistfuls of money. 'Let me to the front!' one merchant was yelling. 'I can pay!'

'How much does a Trade Council guard make, anyway?' a woman behind him shouted. 'Whatever you're getting, I'll double it! Just let me on!'

But the guards stood their ground, heaving the crowd back, ignoring the desperate bribes. Keller was glad of that, though he suspected it would have been a different story if there hadn't been so many people watching.

Someone in the front row yelled in pain as the surging crowd crushed them against the line of guards, who had to shove them back hard.

'Please stay calm,' pleaded the guard captain uselessly. 'Boarding will shortly commence—'

Keller strode up to him and took the voice amplifier out of his hands. He patched it into the planet's public address system. 'This is Trade King Keller speaking!' he said. The crowd fell silent, then began to murmur in astonishment. 'Nobody panic.'

'We need to get on!' a woman screamed. 'You have to take us! We don't have our own ships! We'll be killed!'

'Nobody will be left behind,' Keller promised. 'Bellori ships are willing to take anyone who doesn't have access to another ship. But you have to stay in line!'

'I demand to be allowed on first!' yelled a man dragging a hover-sled piled with bags and boxes. 'I was here before any of them!'

'You will be allowed on in order of arrival,' Keller said. He took a deep breath. 'But passengers only. No luggage is allowed.'

Uproar broke out. Voices screamed at him, begging, pleading, even threatening.

'This is all I have!'

'I've worked all my life for this!'

'We carried this stuff all the way from our house!'

'No luggage!' Keller said sternly. 'You can bring the clothes you're wearing and that is all. This is only a precaution, remember. We'll be coming back soon. All your possessions will be waiting for you here on Cantor.'

That didn't go down at all well. Many of the Cantorians burst into tears. There was fighting among groups as people tried to wrestle bags out of each other's hands. Keller saw fists shaking at him and heard yells of anger, demands to know why they couldn't bring even so much as a handbag.

I owe them an answer for that, at least. 'We need every cubic millipace of space for passengers,' he said. 'And I'm not leaving anyone behind. Your goods can always be replaced. People can't!'

He turned the voice amplifier off and went to join his people. The guards let him through.

The sight of so many miserable faces was hard to bear. All around him, Cantorians were crying as they abandoned the things they'd hoped to keep safe. 'I'll never see them again,' a child was sobbing as her father gently took her toys away and left them in a storage bin.

'Yes you will!' Keller told her. 'As soon as the Bellori have dealt with the nasty aliens, we'll all come straight back home!'

Not long after, the boarding was almost complete. Keller walked among his people, doing his best to calm them prior to take-off. Most people recognized him, but he was surprised how many didn't. It was no longer easy to tell a trade king from a house servant, now that nobody had any possessions.

The Cantorians prepared to head into space, bringing nothing but the clothes on their backs, more equal than they had ever been before.

The few rocky islands on Aquanthis made perfect landing pads for the Bellori evacuation ships. The hatchways stood open, but only a few exhausted Aquanths had climbed aboard so far. Beneath the surface, the rest of the Aquanths were still chanting, keeping groups of Bellori protected as they fought their way to their own ships.

As he stood holding hands with his mother and the rest of the group, forming a circle, Ayl could feel Aquanths wincing and recoiling in horror every time a Bellori blasted a Nara-Karith or sliced through one with a blade.

As more and more Bellori escaped, the Aquanths who had been shielding them were able to withdraw and board the evacuation ships. Ayl could see them in his mind's eye, staggering up the ramps with shell-shocked faces and haggard eyes.

Ship by ship, the Bellori and the Aquanths evacuated their respective worlds. *Our peoples have never been so close*, Ayl thought. *Our escape is a mirror of theirs.*

His mother's hand tightened in his and he heard her groan. Suddenly, a stab of pain shot through his head. A gathering force, dark and deadly, was bearing down on them. He knew that mind all too well.

'It's Sudor!' he said. 'He's fighting back!'

Sudor's voice hissed into the Aquanths' minds: *A clever trick. Almost worthy of a warrior. But it is far too late for the Aquanths to learn courage.*

His mind blasted theirs like a screaming desert gale, tearing at their thoughts with hot, barbed shards of pure agony. The Aquanth connection to the Bellori weakened and began to fray. In Ayl's circle, the chanting faltered.

'I can't hold it!' howled an Aquanth. 'My mind . . . it's burning up!'

'Keep chanting!' Lady Moa said. 'If we let go now, the Bellori are as good as dead!'

You cannot stop me, Sudor gloated. *You do not have the strength.*

An image of Sudor was beginning to appear in the centre of the circle now, formed from pure psychic force. A huge, demonic, half-Bellori half-insect shadow surrounded by flames.

The pressure on Ayl's mind was unbearable, as if the whole weight of Bellus was crushing him. One of the Aquanths screamed out loud, and blood erupted from her mouth. She went limp.

'Don't let go of her hands!' Lady Moa said.

'I think she's dead,' sobbed the Aquanth beside her.

'Don't break the circle! We have to drive him back!'

Together, the Aquanths focused their wills on Sudor. The hands holding Ayl's were vice-tight, agonizing.

Sudor wasn't yielding. One solitary maniac was opposing the entire focused will of Aquanthis. His image was growing clearer and stronger. The connection to Bellus was hanging by a thread.

Your world is next, Sudor gloated. *These waters shall soon run red.*

Suddenly, Ayl knew what he had to do. *He's facing Aquanthis as a single mind – his will deadlocked against our will, like two battlefronts. If I break free of the collective, I can strike his mind where it's undefended! But I'd be exposed . . .*

He felt his mother press his hand into a different Aquanth's grip. She broke away from the circle before he could stop her.

Too late, he knew she'd had the same thought.

'No!' he screamed, fighting against the hands that gripped him.

Lady Moa raised her hands above her head and loosed a blast of mental energy at the Sudor-shape. He gave a piercing mental shriek and began to blur at the edges, like a foulness dissolving into the water.

'Begone, tyrant!' she yelled. 'We cast you out, back to the outer darkness!'

The image wavered and shrank. In that moment Ayl knew she'd done it. The sudden, unexpected attack from a new direction had shattered Sudor's mind control. The Aquanths began chanting with fresh urgency, renewing the link with Bellus, restoring the mental shield.

But as Sudor's presence faded away to nothing, a tentacle of pure focused hate shot out from it and ripped into Lady Moa. It tore her consciousness away and left her floating like a rag doll, drifting at the mercy of the current.

'Mother!'

Ayl desperately tried to link his mind with hers, to bring her back into the collective. *Keller's father, dead. Dray's father, dead. But not her. Please, not her.*

There was nothing in his mother's mind but a cold, dead silence.

* * *

'BELLUS CORE ACTIVITY NORMAL,' droned the computer.

Not for long, Dray thought, feeling a little sick. 'General Mursh, estimated time until boarding complete?'

'No longer than ten clicks, General Dray.' He glanced at her, and she saw how he licked his lips nervously. Had he always been doing that inside his helmet, hidden from view?

Without her armour, Dray thought, she must look like a callow young girl. If any of her council thought so, they had not let it show. They all looked more afraid than anything. If only Dray hadn't stripped them of their armour – but no, she had done the right thing by her people. She knew she had.

'And Sudor? What's he doing?'

'He's in the command centre. Most of his bugs are still tearing Bellus apart to get at the ore. The rest are trying to stop our people evacuating.'

'Show me the evacuations,' she ordered.

At once, the viewscreen changed to display the armourless Bellori fighting their way to the evacuation ships. Dray watched, every muscle tense. Some of the Bellori were cut down and bleeding on to the soil of

Bellus, but many of them made it on to the ships. One after another, ships went roaring up through the stratosphere, away from Sudor, into the safety of space.

'I will build a monument to honour your memory,' Dray whispered to the fallen.

She changed the view on the screens, watching the evacuations in city after city. Now the command bunker was displayed, with a huge mound of some sort of junk close to it. What had the bugs done there? Frowning, Dray increased the magnification.

She saw gauntlets, greaves, breastplates. It was Bellori armour, chucked into a pile like so much trash. She stared at it, hatred of Sudor rising like bile inside her, and waited for the confirmation that the evacuation was complete.

It wasn't long in coming. 'All ships departed, General Dray,' said Mursh.

'Do any Bellori remain on Bellus?' Dray had to know.

'None. All survivors are accounted for.'

So. For the first time, Bellus was truly defenceless. All her protectors were gone.

Dray cracked her knuckles. 'Coms, hail the command bunker. I want to speak to Sudor himself. And tell the Aquanths they can stand down, with my thanks. We owe them our lives today.'

The viewscreen dissolved in static. Moments later, the image of the main control centre appeared, still partially destroyed from the battle. Sudor stood, clicking his pincers against his chest armour and laughing at her.

'Trying to earn your place in the history books again, Dray? I have heard of cowards abandoning their posts, but never of one so cowardly she abandoned her entire planet.'

Gloat while you can, you filth.

'Listen to my words carefully, traitor,' said Dray. 'The Bellori fleet stands ready. On my command, they will begin bombing. The bombing will not stop until we have confirmation of your death. However, I am still willing to accept your unconditional surrender.'

Sudor laughed long and hard. 'That bluff was played out last time you tried it! Have you forgotten I am a Bellori too?' He leaned in, sneering. 'I *know* about the planet's unstable core. You aren't going to bomb a target on Bellus, Dray, even if all your people have fled. You wouldn't risk it.'

'This is your last chance,' Dray said. 'Do you surrender?'

'Never,' Sudor said, 'and especially not to a weakling

like you.' He held his hands up, palms upward. 'There. The game's over, little girl. What will you do now?'

Dray opened a coms channel. 'All ships, this is General Dray.'

'Reading you. Go ahead, General.'

She closed her eyes. Her stomach was a tight hard knot, but her voice was firm and clear. 'Stand by for my bombing order.'

16

Lady Moa's eyes opened. She looked up from the rock pool where she lay, then sank back down, her gills pulsing.

'Ayl?' she said weakly. 'Where are we?'

'On a landing pad.' Ayl looked around at the ships, where lines of Aquanths were filing on board. 'You're going to be taken on to a Bellori ship soon, but the healers said to keep you in water for as long as possible.'

'I remember. Yes. The Bellori. How many of them lived?' she said through pale lips.

'Most of them. Most of them made it. General Dray sent her personal thanks.'

'And Sudor?'

Ayl hesitated. 'Still alive. For now.'

'Look,' she said, sounding very old and frail. 'There's Wan.'

The youth was moving up one of the queues, along with the rest of Ayl's old circle of friends.

Ayl caught Wan's eye. *How is she?* Wan asked him telepathically.

The healers say she'll be OK, he replied. *But it was close.*

I'll pray for her, Wan assured him. *And for you.*

Hard to believe you're finally going to travel beyond Aquanthis, Ayl thought, changing the subject. *Ready to have your mind broadened forever?*

Wan smiled. *I know! Me, on a spaceship! Can you imagine it?*

Promise me one thing, Ayl joked. *If you get space-sick, don't mind-link with me.*

Don't worry, Wan said. *If you can get used to it, I'm sure I can.*

Keep safe, podbrother. Ayl smiled, but his tone was serious. *You'll be in my prayers.*

And you'll be in mine, Wan sent back. *See you on the other side of the sky.*

Ayl watched Wan disappear into the belly of the ship. He hoped Wan would get a taste for space travel. Perhaps one day, when all this was over, they would explore the stars together.

Then he looked out over the beckoning ocean and sighed. No. It didn't seem likely. Wan would always have Aquanthis to come back to, and under the skin he was as resistant to change as any other Aquanth.

The lines had gone down and now only two ships were left. A group of Aquanth elders, led by the Naptarch, came and stood by him. Lady Moa was sleeping in her rock pool now, looking small and shrunken.

'We need to take her with us,' the Naptarch said.

'She's not coming with me on my ship? I thought we'd be travelling together.'

The Naptarch shook his head. 'The Bellori won't allow it. They need the high priestess and her heir to travel separately, in case there's an accident or an attack. Can't risk losing both of you.' He glanced balefully at the guards. 'Always practical, the Bellori. Always willing to imagine the worst.'

Ayl leaned down and kissed Lady Moa on her cold cheek.

'May we meet again, mother,' he said.

'If it is fated, you will,' the Naptarch replied. Then the group of Aquanths lifted the high priestess gently and carried her on to the waiting ship. Moments later, its engines ignited and it rose into the sky.

The sea all around was empty and still. Ayl looked up at the last remaining ship. Its boarding ramp was empty too, but for the Bellori standing guard. One of them inclined his head, telling Ayl it was time to leave.

I'm the last.

He went to board the ship, but hesitated. Suddenly he turned and swam full tilt off into the sea. The guards looked at one another.

A few clicks later, he came swimming back, exhausted. Under his arm he carried the stone tablet on which the prophecy was engraved.

'We're good to go,' he gasped to the guards.

The Trade Council guard captain watched, fidgeting, as Keller piloted the Bellori battle cruiser out of Cantor's atmosphere. From the cabin behind them came the hubbub of hundreds of Cantorians chatting, bickering, laughing and arguing.

Well, Keller thought, *I did decide to spend more time among my people. This wasn't quite what I had in mind, though . . .*

Keller was glad the Bellori crew had given over the controls to him without a word of protest. Now, if only this idiot would stop fretting and let him concentrate! What was he so worried about? Keller might be flying a little faster than most passengers were used to, but there was no sense in dawdling.

'Something on your mind?' Keller eventually snapped.

'You're flying this ship above the recommended safe speed!' the guard captain burst out.

'Don't worry. I know what I'm doing.'

'But we're endangering the evacuees!'

'We're safer up here than we would be on Cantor.' *Especially with me at the controls, you cretin.* 'Go and make yourself useful. Get some ration packs from the storage locker and hand them out to the passengers. They must be hungry.'

Keller adjusted the screen to show a view of Bellus. He couldn't let Dray go through this alone. He had to see what she was seeing. Even if all he could do was watch on a display screen.

Suddenly, a brilliant flash came from Bellus's surface, bathing the cockpit in white light. Two more explosions quickly followed, rippling blasts of orange and red.

A chorus of 'oohs' and 'aahs' came from the passengers, as if they were watching fireworks. They were watching Bellus too, he realized.

'They must have started the bombardment,' Keller murmured to himself. 'Give Sudor hell, Dray. Finish him.'

Points of light were appearing all across the surface of Bellus, along with hairline cracks of crimson fire. That must be the planet's molten mantle, bursting through the ravaged crust. 'Hold together, Bellus,' he whispered.

What kind of a home would the Bellori have to go back to? Keller wondered. He cycled the display through different ground-level views of Bellus. Each one told the same story. Bellus had always been rugged and inhospitable, but now even the cities and encampments were in ruins. With the Bellori gone, the Nara-Karith were ripping the world apart, plundering everything. Keller suspected Sudor was wreaking destruction for the sheer joy of it.

He felt gutted, as if a Nara-Karith limb had jabbed into his stomach and ripped his insides out. Even after all the victories he, Ayl and Dray had won, Bellus was in flames. It hardly seemed worth it now.

If this is hard for me to watch, what must Dray be going through? he thought.

He pressed his hand against the cold viewscreen, thinking of Dray out there on the bridge, forced to watch her commands carried out. Just for a moment, he wished he had Ayl's gift of telepathy. *I could reach out to her, touch her mind. Just so she wouldn't have to do this alone.*

He had no way to reach her. He let his hand fall. The gulf of space had never seemed darker or colder.

'Deep fried falchort wings in zetaspice! There you go, sir! Nicer than Bellori ration packs, eh?'

The voice had come from the passenger section. Keller angrily set the ship to autopilot and went through to see this for himself.

He could hardly believe it. A trader had rigged up a food stall in the middle of the passenger aisle. Boxes full of luxury goodies lay open – candies, snacks, containers of lumojuice – and the hastily applied price stickers were ten times the usual Cantor price. Judging by the crowd gathered around him, people were all too eager to buy.

Keller looked around for the Trade Council guard captain, and saw him quickly hiding something wrapped in paper behind his back. His cheeks were bulging. He stared at Keller like a startled hamster, too frightened to chew.

The trader turned round, saw Keller, and gave a cheery grin. 'Care for a box of chocolates, Your Majesty?'

'What the krack is this?' Keller said quietly, and all the voices around him died down to a whisper.

'Uh . . . free enterprise?'

'Where are the Bellori ration packs?' Keller asked the guard captain.

'Gone,' the guard captain said. 'It seems they were unloaded before take-off. This gentlemen said he was handling the catering.'

The trader held his hands up. 'Come on, Your Majesty. Be reasonable. You can't expect Cantorians to eat Bellori military rations, can you?'

'Let me get this straight, you mullock,' Keller said. 'You dumped the free rations so you could set up a stall and charge people money for food?'

'Yeah, well,' the trader blustered. 'Can't blame a man for seizing an opportunity, can you? I mean, *trade* is what it's all about, isn't that right?' He winked and shoved the box of sweets into Keller's hands. 'Go on. I've heard you like 'em, Trade King. On the house.'

Keller passed the box to the guard captain. 'Place this man under arrest. He can spend the rest of the journey in the brig.'

'But . . . but . . .' the trader spluttered. 'My merchandise!'

'Oh yes,' said Keller. 'Share this food out to everyone on board. All of it. Equally. At no charge.'

The guard captain dragged the yelling trader away. The Cantorian passengers looked on in awed silence. Keller hadn't finished with them yet.

'All of you,' he said, 'look at the screens. Look at Bellus, the planet where our neighbours live. The ones who protect us. Their home is being destroyed right in front of you. This is not in-flight entertainment! People are dying.'

Dray's flagship flew above a world tormented with fire, shrouded with smoke. The hills had deep gouges torn into them, the bunkers were shattered ruins. The evacuation had come at a terrible cost.

She couldn't think about that now. She had to keep her mind on the prey.

'BELLUS CORE ACTIVITY ABNORMAL,' the computer warned. 'INSTABILITY EIGHTEEN PER CENT AND RISING.'

'Reading a jamming attempt from the command centre,' said the communications officer, sounding confused. 'They're trying to override our controls, but the cyphers are all wrong. All systems responding normally.'

Thanks for that, Keller, Dray thought. She imagined Sudor's fury when he found his control overrides weren't working, and allowed herself a grin.

'Sudor's ship in range!' the helmsman said.

Next moment she saw it, looming on the skyline, towering over the command bunker like a nightmare given form.

'Request confirmation that evacuation of Cantor and Aquanthis is complete,' she barked into her com-link.

'Affirmative: both planets now clear,' came the reply.

'All weapons, target Sudor's ship!' she ordered. 'Concentrate fire on the midsection!'

'Plasma cannon banks armed and ready. Missiles primed.'

'FIRE!'

The full firepower of the mightiest ship in the Bellori fleet thundered and blazed. Rank upon brilliant rank of plasma charges slammed into the dark ship's hull, followed by the deeper, booming detonations of missiles.

'That should soften him up,' Dray said. 'Lock target for bombing run.'

Three short beeps sounded, and the console trilled. 'We have lock!' called the gunner.

Dray nodded. 'Squash him like a bug.'

208

Bombs fell, silver and silent, through the smoke clouds.

Blossoms of incinerating light too bright to look at spread out below the flagship, which rocked wildly as the shockwave hit. The explosions were astounding, as if an angel of hellfire had spread its wings beneath the sky.

Nothing could withstand that kind of onslaught for long. Armour plating disintegrated into fragments, and the metal skeleton beneath glowed and buckled. Conduits burst, releasing steam and burning gases. Whole sections of the ship's surface suddenly exploded from beneath in fountains of fire, scattering white-hot fragments like counters from an overturned gameboard.

Dray tightened her fist.

Then the whole craft shook as one of the legs, pounded beyond endurance, burst open at the joint like a blocked rifle barrel. The separated leg toppled, falling slowly as a demolished tower, crushing countless Nara-Karith as it fell.

With a groan like something dying, the immense ship toppled sideways. Now other legs were buckling, giving way under the weight. The earth shook as the whole centre section crashed down, taking part of the command bunker with it.

Dray held her breath. *Was Sudor in there?*

'General Dray! Incoming com . . .' The helmsman looked up. 'It's Sudor.'

Dray leapt forwards. 'On the main screen!'

The view was at an angle, as if the impact had knocked the camera askew. The command room was a burning caved-in ruin. Flames leaped inside shattered computer monitors.

Sudor clutched towards the screen with an outstretched hand. He was helmetless. 'Dray,' he gasped.

Dray saw a huge girder had fallen across him, pinning him down. His multiple limbs were twitching. Some had broken and dangled useless. He looked like a dying insect.

'You . . . are a coward,' he gasped painfully, and forced out a laugh. 'Your blood is weak, girl. You are so selfish that you've endangered your whole world . . . just to kill me!'

'INSTABILITY AT THIRTY PER CENT AND RISING,' the computer clanged.

Sudor laughed again as he heard it. 'You will not go through with this! You . . . do not . . . have the COURAGE!' He spat the word out.

'I should have done this a long time ago,' Dray said bitterly. 'Firehawks, begin second attack wave.'

'Locked and ready!' came the voice of the squadron leader. The V-shaped wing of Firehawks came roaring over the horizon.

Dray bit her lip as they approached. They were almost above Sudor's ship – and the command bunker – now. Defiant to the last, Sudor was laughing louder and louder.

'Finish him!' Dray ordered.

The Firehawks loosed their astron charges.

Dray hung on to the rail, her eyes fixed on the viewscreen. The view through the camera shook crazily. She heard Sudor scream and struggle.

Just then, the command centre vanished in a roaring inferno of blue-white light. Shockwaves pummelled the whole area and typhoon winds rocked the flagship. On the screen, she saw Sudor's body glow and turn to ash as a wave of purifying fire engulfed the room. Then the image dissolved into chaos.

Dray stared at the static dancing on the screen for several clicks, still clinging to the rail as if she would crumple if she let it go. She had no words for what she was feeling right now. The relief she felt at Sudor's death was sweeter than samthorn wine, and the thrill of victory made her head spin, but there was a bitter rage, too. His death would not bring back the fallen.

Nobody on the bridge said a word. The flagship flew over the shattered landscape of Bellus, and nothing but destruction lay all around.

'INSTABILITY AT FORTY-NINE PER CENT AND RISING.'

Dray touched her arm, remembering the blood oath she had sworn to kill Sudor. Now, at last, it was done. She'd had revenge. But there was no pleasure in it, not when the cost was so high. For so long she had sworn to savour this moment, and now it was turning to ashes, just like her homeworld.

A group of buildings caught her eye, next to a familiar-looking mountain. *That's the barracks where I live*, she suddenly thought. *My room, my bed, all my things, in that tiny group of bunkers.*

For a moment she thought it might have escaped intact, but as the flagship passed overhead, she saw the smoking, shattered remains of the barracks lay open to the burning sky.

Dray felt cold inside. She had ridden on her father's shoulders around those blackened shells.

Perhaps it was a mercy that General Iccus was dead. At least he hadn't lived to see this day.

'Can't you do anything about this?' the Bellori pilot demanded.

Ayl glanced behind him. The groans and sobs coming from the Aquanth passengers were getting louder and louder. It was like being in a hospital ward.

The pilot shook his head. 'One space-sick passenger, I can handle. Two is a pain. But a whole shipload? This makes a tour of duty in the swamps of Tra-Zangh seem like a picnic.'

'They can't help it!' Ayl snapped defensively.

'Is that a fact? You seem to be handling space travel well enough.'

'Yeah, well, I'm used to it,' Ayl said. 'Look, I'll talk to them, OK? Let me see what I can do.'

He opened the door to the passenger compartments. Row upon row of suffering Aquanths sat groaning in their seats. Some looked up at him with miserable faces, pleading silently for him to help. The rest just clutched their stomachs and moaned, or stared in horror at the viewscreen set above the aisle. Many of them were crying hysterically.

This was more than just space-sickness. These Aquanths looked terrified. Ayl looked up at the viewscreen and understood why.

It showed a live feed from Bellus. Volcanic eruptions were tearing the surface of the planet apart. Nara-Karith were burning, dying in their thousands. All their lives, these Aquanths had been sheltered from violence. Now they were drowning in it.

Ayl quickly turned the viewscreen off, but still the sobs and shudders went on. He understood why. Only moments ago, these Aquanths had shielded the Bellori as they fought their way off the planet. They'd seen a lifetime's worth of violence in one day.

He reached out to them with his mind. *Listen, all of you*, he urged. *We need to band together and get through this. Link minds with me!*

At first they ignored him, paralysed by horror and nausea. Ayl persisted. One by one, tentative but trusting, they linked their minds to his.

Good, he said. *We need to pray together for the safety of the Trinity System. Don't think about yourselves. Forget what your bodies are feeling. Focus on the spirit, and pray with me.*

The Aquanths began to chant. Ayl encountered each of their minds in turn and soothed them as best he could, calming their fears, helping them to meditate. Everything they were suffering, from the gut-wrenching misery of space-sickness to the terror of war, Ayl had already suffered and overcome long ago.

It was a strange and wonderful calm, this feeling of showing others the way. All his own suffering had been worth it, because now he could help others. If he hadn't undergone those ordeals, he'd have been as helpless as they were now.

I feel sick! a little Aquanth protested, when it was her turn. *We keep wobbling about!*

Don't worry, Ayl explained. *It's only turbulence. It'll stop when we get into space.*

He felt her mind grow calmer. *It is! It's stopping already!*

So, they were finally out of the atmosphere and on their way into space. Ayl let himself relax a little.

Suddenly, a shockwave slammed into the ship. Ayl heard the pilot yelling something about an explosion. He lunged for a safety grip, but the ship was already spinning wildly, flinging the helpless Aquanths this way and that.

Oh please no, not now I've got them calmed down!

But the damage was done.

There was an unmistakable *hork*. And then another.

And another. One by one, in a messy, revolting chain reaction, the Aquanths threw up in their laps.

17

Volcanic eruptions burst again and again across the surface of Bellus. Core instability was at fifty-nine per cent and rising.

'That's way beyond any previous recorded level!' Scraa told Dray, his face pale and haggard. 'The bombs destabilized the core. We warned you this would happen!'

'What are the Nara-Karith doing?' Dray demanded.

The science officer tapped buttons. 'It looks like they're going crazy, General. Groups of them are fighting one another. Without Sudor's leadership, they're running amok.'

'Good. We wait for the core to stabilize, then we land the ships and finish them hand-to-hand.'

The other generals nodded vigorously.

'General?' said the coms officer. 'There's something you need to see.' He pointed to a waveform on the screen. 'Just when Sudor died, an automated transmission was sent to his ship.'

'What sort of transmission?'

'I can't quite tell – but it looks like a security code.'

'CORE INSTABILITY AT FIFTY-EIGHT PER CENT AND FALLING,' tolled the computer suddenly.

Cheers rang out across the bridge, and the generals slapped each other on the back. 'Did you hear that?' Mursh crowed. 'The core's stabilizing! We can go home!'

'Bellus has endured,' said Tothin solemnly. 'Bellus shall endure forever.'

'We've won,' Brancur said. 'This day shall be your day forever, Dray daughter of Iccus.'

Dray ignored him.

Brancur began to sing an ancient Bellori marching song, and some of the other generals joined in. From across the bridge Vayne looked on, silent, fearful, refusing to celebrate. It gave Dray the terrible feeling that something was very wrong.

Dray looked at the cryptic waveform on the screen, wishing it would give up its secrets. Why had Sudor sent an automated transmission? Why bother? It wouldn't be any use after he was dead.

Unless . . .

The helmsman jumped up with a yell. 'General! Sudor's ship – it's going critical!'

'What? On screen, *now*!'

The tilted wreck of the spider-ship appeared on the screen. A searing, unexpected light was shining through the armour plating in the main body.

'Something's triggered a chain reaction in the main reactor,' stammered the helmsman. 'Readings are off the scale. It's going to blow.'

Dray stared at the waveform and suddenly understood. Even in death, Sudor would never accept defeat. All it would take was a simple transmitter, linked to his armour, monitoring his vital signs. So if he was killed, his ship could deliver one final punishment from beyond the grave . . .

'Sudor!' Dray screamed. 'He's triggered the self-destruct!'

The light came spearing through the spider-ship's casing in blinding rays. Nara-Karith writhed on the ground nearby, then shrivelled in the intense heat. The light became too bright to look at – and then the ship exploded.

Dray looked out of the window at Bellus. The explosion was clearly visible from space. It fanned out across the planet's surface, tearing up the land and turning it to white-hot ash.

'By all the ancestors!' said Brancur in awe.

Dray had never seen an explosion so huge. Compared to that continent-spanning blast, the Bellori fusion bombs had been pinpricks.

'All pilots, leave the area as fast as you can!' she yelled into her communicator. 'Repeat, *clear the area*!'

Mursh pointed with a shaking hand. 'Look.'

The core instability gauge was a solid bar of red. 'CORE INSTABILITY NINETY-NINE POINT FIVE PER CENT,' the computer barked. 'EVACUATE. EVACUATE. EVACUATE.'

'That last explosion,' Brancur said hollowly. 'The size of it . . .'

'General, I'm reading unprecedented seismic activity on Bellus!' the helmsman said. 'Earthquakes in all regions, volcanic eruptions, fissures opening . . .'

A fountain of red sprayed up from Bellus's surface, as if the planet had been gashed to the heart. Another volcano erupted immediately afterwards, hurling molten lava all the way into space. Gases trapped for millions of turns seethed up as the planet cracked like a colossal egg, traceries of fiery red spreading out and growing brighter.

'The planet's going!' howled the gunnery officer.

'What can we do?' screamed one of the generals. 'General, what can we do?

Dray had no answer to give.

'All ships, fall back!' she ordered desperately. 'Retreat out of planetary range!'

The Bellori watched Bellus raging, holding their breath. Dray's eyes were fixed on the gauge, which quivered at ninety-nine point five per cent.

The fleet came streaming up away from Bellus, with a volley of flying rock fragments close behind. The com channels still open to the surface relayed a deafening rumble, as if the world were ripping itself apart at the seams.

Please, Dray thought, *if there is anything out there that can hear me, please, let my world survive.*

The planet rumbled ominously and jetted flame and smoke, coughed one last gigantic spume of lava into the void, and then fell abruptly silent. The instability gauge hovered a few critical pixels below one hundred per cent.

Clicks of silence passed.

Slowly, almost imperceptibly, the instability gauge began to climb down. 'INSTABILITY AT NINETY-NINE PER CENT AND FALLING,' the computer confirmed.

Dray closed her eyes and breathed a sigh of relief. All around her, the generals did the same. *It's over. Even after that, Bellus is safe. All of Trinity is safe. Thank the ancestors.*

A shattering roar filled the bridge. Dray's eyes flew open.

Mammoth cracks were opening up in Bellus's crust. Seas of lava were boiling over, engulfing the land. The whole planet was trembling violently. Surge after surge of molten matter came bursting up from the planet's tormented core, fountaining into space.

'No!' The word came out as a strangled sob.

Then, for a click, the darkness of space was suddenly lit by a brand new sun as Bellus exploded into trillions of burning fragments.

As Keller steered his craft away from Bellus at top speed, he didn't even have time to be horrified. *Bellus is gone*, he thought. In its place there was only a storm of rocky debris, many times larger than the original planet.

He stared at the oncoming huge cloud of fragments travelling terrifyingly fast towards him. Then all of a sudden his ship was plunging into it.

He swerved to avoid a chunk of Bellus. It came so

close that he could make out the remains of buildings on one side. The ship's controls shuddered in his hands. There was a hollow clang as something glanced off the hull.

He wiped his sweating forehead. More pieces of Bellus were hurtling towards him like missiles. He could hear the ship's passengers screaming. He lurched the ship upwards and then sharply down like a rollercoaster, narrowly avoiding a fatal collision.

Dray's lost her homeworld, he thought, and his heart sank. He couldn't imagine what she was going through right now. After everything she'd done, everything she'd sacrificed – it was too cruel. She might try to put on a brave face, but Keller knew she would never be the same again. Dray had loved her planet. This would shatter her, break her heart beyond repair.

No time to worry about that now, he told himself. He swerved, rolled and banked, fighting to keep the ship intact.

The remains of Bellus were coming thick and fast, and there was something else going on out there, something that was sending the instruments haywire. The ship was flung from side to side, the controls bucking in Keller's hands.

'Like flying through a storm,' Keller muttered.

'But that's not possible! There's no atmosphere out there!'

He thumped the instrument panel, to no avail. According to his screens, there were weird fluctuations in gravity going on around him. Odd waves and currents – things that shouldn't be happening.

'Must be something to do with Bellus blowing up,' he said to himself.

Then a fist-like mass of rock came hurtling out of the darkness. Keller slammed on full retro thrust and just managed to sideswipe out of the way. More screams, and a few desperate prayers, came from the passengers.

Keller decided he had had enough. They would have been safer back on Cantor. 'OK, people, evacuation's over!' he yelled. 'We're going home!'

He heard cheering, and smiled. He reached over to the navigation panel with one hand, steering with the other. They'd soon be back on Cantor and out of this mess.

His home planet appeared against the starfield on the panel, moving rapidly through space towards his current position. Good. That would make for a shorter jump.

Keller turned back to his flying, then spun back

around to stare at the navigation panel as he realized what he'd just seen.

'What?' he yelled. 'WHAT?'

Either he had gone completely mad, or Cantor was changing position. He blinked, rubbed his eyes, and stared. There could be no doubt about it. His homeworld had slipped out of its usual orbit and was heading in this direction, picking up speed as it went.

'Holy krack,' he whispered.

Then something wrenched at the ship with the strength of a titan. *Gravity wave*, Keller just had time to think, before everything went black.

All at once, the Aquanths on Ayl's ship stopped chanting.

Ayl listened. No sound at all came from the passenger compartments. The utter, terrified silence made him deeply uneasy. *What have they sensed?*

'No, no, no!' the Bellori pilot was saying as he fumbled with the controls. 'This cannot be happening!'

'Calm down!' said Ayl, doing his best to send out a telepathic wave of peace. 'What's wrong?'

The pilot was too frightened to answer. He pointed up at the navigation screen.

Ayl instantly saw the horrific truth. Bellus had been

destroyed, leaving behind a swarming mass of asteroids. A stab of pain went through him as he thought of Dray. But even that tragedy was not what was terrifying the pilot – or the Aquanth passengers.

When Bellus had exploded, the three planets of the Trinity System had been in alignment. Ayl remembered how his mother had spoken of that great event as a chance for peace. But what the screen showed was as far from peace as it was possible to get.

Cantor and Aquanthis had been dragged out of their orbital paths and were moving towards each other! They were picking up speed even as Ayl watched. Now the remains of Bellus were moving, too, reaching out to both the other planets with arms of fire, dust and debris.

'We're going to die,' the pilot sobbed. 'My wife . . . my planet . . . it's all over.'

I've never felt calmer, Ayl thought, looking down at the hapless man. *How strange.*

He knew this was the end. The three planets of Trinity were being destroyed together in front of him. And yet, his heart felt clear and full of light.

This is it! he thought. *My entire life has led me here. This is destiny. The moment where everything changes!*

The prophecy on its stone tablet was propped

against the wall. Ayl saw its three circles were streaming with light, one blue, one green, one red. From far away, he thought he heard ancient voices singing in harmony.

Of course, he thought, and smiled. *So simple. Why didn't I see it sooner . . .*

The cabin lit up in a blaze of brilliant light, radiating from the stone tablet. Three beams of radiance poured from it, lancing through the darkness of space to where the three planets of the Trinity System were coming together.

On the screen, Aquanthis was changing shape. Ayl felt waves of stark, primal terror emanating from the passengers. They were literally frightened out of their minds, huddling together telepathically as one in the face of their world's end.

He wanted to reach out to them, to reassure them, but could only stare at the screen with wonder in his eyes as the planets came racing towards one another.

Aquanthis was no longer a sphere now. The gravitational forces that were hauling it out of orbit were reshaping it on its journey. The planet was breaking up, splitting into watery orbs, comets and great spaceborne oceans.

The light from the ancient tablet was blinding now.

Ayl's mind was filled with wonder. What distant, star-wandering race had created an artefact that could do this? Had the violent explosion of Bellus awakened it somehow? Or had its creators known this moment was coming, and prepared the tablet for that day? He marvelled at the sheer power the ancients must have had, the power to reshape whole worlds, maybe even whole systems . . .

Ayl heard a warning beep. The pilot was frozen in fear, unable to work the controls. The short-range scanner showed a vast rolling wave of water, once a part of Aquanthis, coming up fast to engulf the ship.

Ayl smiled and raised his hands in welcome. The pilot looked up at him as if he had gone mad.

The wave struck.

18

Dray and her generals watched from the bridge, silent and horrified beyond words. What could any of them possibly say? First their own world, and now the two other worlds of Trinity, were being destroyed forever.

Slowly, as if to spare no detail of the disaster, Cantor ploughed into two enormous whirling masses of debris that had been planets only moments before. One was mostly orange rocks – that had been Bellus. The other was tumbling chunks of ice and rippling globes of water, all that now remained of Aquanthis.

Cantor's gravitational field began to drag the ruined planets down in a deadly hail of wreckage. The very shapes of the landmasses began to change. No navigator would recognize Cantor now, Dray thought. The Nara-Karith's ravaging of Bellus was nothing compared to this devastation.

Tears flooded down Dray's cheeks. It didn't matter

who saw them now. All she could think was how *close* they had come.

We found peace, the three of us, after so long. Our people worked together, supported each other, stood together against a common foe. For once, we were really united, and it felt like the way it should have been all along. We were on the edge of a better tomorrow . . .

And then our own planets destroyed one another.

'Computer, show me Cantor's surface,' she forced herself to say.

I have to see for myself, she thought. *I need to know how bad it is.*

She saw the magnificent cities of Cantor smashed, as fragments of Bellus screamed down from the sky and burst like bombs. Buildings fell, then were buried under mountains of rocky debris. The entire mass of Bellus was hurling itself at Cantor, demolishing farms, incinerating forests, leaving vast craters where fields once stood. No act of war could ever have come close to this.

The people of Cantor might have evacuated, but the animals were not so lucky. Herd beasts in their fields were roasted alive. Falchorts tried to flee from burning forests, only to fall out of the sky with their feathers flaming.

Dray changed the view to show different parts of Cantor, where Aquanthis was raining down on the planet. Colossal walls of water surged through marketplaces and shopping malls, shattering windows and washing trade goods away. Whole forests were swept away in the deluge. The planet was being buried, drowned and burned all at the same time.

She sat looking at the screen for a long time, hypnotized by the devastation, while the tears dried on her face. Smoke and fog were making it harder and harder to see what was happening. Eventually she rose and looked out through the window at the converging worlds, and understood. Massive clouds of white vapour were swirling up into the atmosphere, the result of lava from Bellus plunging into water from Aquanthis.

'Keller,' she whispered hoarsely. 'I'm so sorry.'

The continents were unrecognizable – the forests, lakes and mountain ranges gone. She could not even tell where the cities of the old Cantor had been any more. Mercifully, the vapour from the waters of Aquanthis was covering the devastated planet now, obscuring it beneath a layer of cloud.

She knew what Sudor would say. In her head, she could hear the words as clearly as if he were speaking them now. *Bravo. I salute you, Dray. I see now you were the true master all along! You have achieved more than I ever could. All three worlds of Trinity, destroyed in a single instant. Think of all the homeless children to come, born on scattered outlying worlds and cramped, miserable military outposts. Think of the stories their parents will tell them of you, the great Destroyer. You will be hated, despised, more than any other Bellori in history.*

But nobody could have hated Dray more than she hated herself just then. This was all her doing. She had stripped Bellus of its troops. She had ordered the bombing. She had failed to kill the man who had gone on to cause her planet's destruction. How could she go on living, with so much shame and dishonour on her shoulders?

Her hand went to the hilt of her *scratha* knife. A Bellori leader who failed her people should die by her own hand. There would be pain, but a moment's agony was better than a lifetime's shame. She would fall on her blade in front of her generals.

Then she hesitated.

No. Dying would be the coward's way out. Whatever else I may be, I am no coward.

She released the knife, choosing to live.

'NEW PLANET STABILIZING,' said the

computer with a triumphant beep.

Dray stared, unable to believe it. 'That's impossible!'

The computer began to rattle off statistics: 'ATMOSPHERE BREATHABLE. LAND AREA FIFTY-SIX PER CENT AND RISING. PLANT LIFE: CURRENTLY EMERGENT. ANIMAL LIFE: CURRENTLY EMERGENT.'

'L-life?' Dray stammered. 'That can't be happening, it would take millions of turns.' The computer's circuits must have taken damage, she decided. Nothing could have survived what she'd seen out there.

'MICROCELLULAR LIFE DETECTED,' the computer insisted. 'SPECIES DIVERSIFICATION OBSERVED. NEW PLANET UNDERGOING HYPERACCELERATED EVOLUTION.'

'What's causing it?' Dray demanded.

'UNKNOWN TECHNOLOGY,' the computer said unhelpfully.

'How has that planet stabilized so fast?'

'UNKNOWN TECHNOLOGY,' repeated the computer.

Dray jerked her head around to stare at the new planet again. It was still veiled by thick, impenetrable clouds, which boiled and seethed like the fumes of a cauldron. As she watched, gaps in the clouds began to appear, and the veil steadily dissolved like a conjuring trick.

Something incredible was unfolding before her eyes. The devastation had somehow been transformed into a rebirth. She saw new coastlines, new continents. The display screen showed mountains, valleys, great rolling plains and craggy cliffs. There were outcrops of rock as red as Bellus, seas of Aquanthis blue, and even tiny spots of what must be primitive vegetation, as green as Cantor.

Still the clouds rolled back, uncovering the newborn planet like the unveiling of a magnificent work of art. The computer flooded the screen with statistics, telling anyone who cared to read them of the new world's fertile soil, the abundant minerals, the lifegiving rivers and streams.

'What *is* this?' General Scraa said in awe. 'It's . . . it's like . . .'

'Like the birth of a new world,' Dray said, numb from shock.

She remembered how scornful she'd been of Ayl and his precious prophecy. But she suspected, as she surveyed the new landscapes, that some higher power had been at work here, something Ayl had perhaps understood better than any of them. Bellori didn't believe in miracles, but she couldn't deny what she was seeing with her own two eyes.

'NEW PLANET REACHING FULL STABILITY,' announced the computer.

The Bellori stood and watched in amazed silence as the new world knit itself together in front of them.

General Mursh handed Dray a cup of steaming nutri-broth. 'You look like you could use it,' he said.

When the computer was sure the planet was stable, everyone looked to Dray expectantly. She stood up, still marvelling at the new world before them.

'I guess we had better go investigate,' she said. 'Does anyone *not* want to volunteer?'

Moments later, a Bellori Firehawk touched down on the surface of the newly forged world. The blast jets raised great clouds of dust. Dray wondered which planet the dust had once been part of. All three, perhaps.

The computer had said the atmosphere was breathable. Dray extended the ramp and took her first steps on to the surface of the new planet. She stamped down experimentally, finding it firm. The dust tickled her throat, making her cough. Through the dust clouds, she could make out the rough shapes of hills in the distance, and a jagged silhouette on the skyline that might once have been a city.

For better or for worse, she thought, *this is home now.*

Keller's first conscious thought was *ouch*. His head ached as if a gang of Bellori had been using it for a football.

He was lying face-down on a cold surface. It reminded him very much of the time he'd thrown a victory party after winning the Hazodrene Cup and had woken up inside the laundry droid. He couldn't remember how he'd got there, and on reflection decided he was probably better off not knowing.

He rubbed his eyes. *That was one heck of a dream*, he thought. *Planets exploding, zooming out of orbit, slamming into one another . . . OK, better get breakfast and call a cleaner to sort out the mess. There's bound to be a mess. There always is.*

He sat up and looked around.

Yes, this was a mess all right. Instead of a ship's cockpit, he was sitting in a cramped hollow of mangled metal. Broken cables dangled from the ceiling.

Oh krack. It wasn't a dream. He remembered the ship spinning out of control now. No wonder his head was aching. After a crash like that, he was lucky to be alive.

The pilot's yoke was lying on the floor, ripped off by the force of the impact. *We must have landed on autopilot,* Keller thought in horror. *But where are we?*

And what about the passengers? Keller's jaw fell open as he turned and saw the rest of the ship wasn't there. His end of the ship had been torn off in the crash! The corridor that should have led through to the passenger compartment was blocked with fallen junk.

'Your Majesty?' yelled a gruff, familiar voice. 'Can you hear me?'

Keller grinned. He was actually glad to hear Tyrus for once. Today was turning into one miracle after another. 'Yes! I'm fine!'

'Thank the Gods!' Yall shouted from somewhere outside. 'Everyone, over here! Help clear the debris out of the way!'

'He's alive!' roared Tyrus. 'Trade King Keller is alive!'

Tyrus and Yall pulled the fallen junk out of the way from outside, clearing a space just wide enough for Keller to crawl through. He winced as he pulled himself out into the daylight. *I could have sworn that gap was wider . . .*

There were Cantorians there, but not the ones he'd flown with. 'Where are the other passengers from my ship?' he demanded, getting to his feet. 'Are they all right?' He badly needed to know what planet they had landed on – this obviously wasn't Cantor – but that could wait.

'This way,' Tyrus said.

The broken-off rear section of the ship lay a short walk away, and Keller's blood ran cold as he saw the shattered stump of the nose. He felt very glad to be alive.

With help from Yall and Tyrus, he cleared the ship's emergency exit and helped the passengers out. They stumbled into the sunlight, coughing, crying, thanking everything they could think of that they were alive.

'Thank the Bellori, if you want to thank anyone,' Keller joked as they helped the last survivor out. 'It was their gelfield technology that saved us. Emergency personal forcefields that kick in when a ship crashes. Clever, really.'

Tyrus nodded gravely. 'We can only hope others have survived, too. We detected other ships landing, but we lost track of them.'

Keller suddenly thought of Dray and Ayl. Could they still be alive? It seemed too much to hope for. One more miracle on a day of miracles.

He frowned. 'Where *are* we, anyway?'

Yall and Tyrus exchanged glances. 'You don't know?'

'Last thing I remember was a gravity wave hauling the ship off course. Then I blacked out. The ship landed on autopilot. What? Did I miss something?'

'Well,' Tyrus began, 'it seems the three planets have . . . converged. It sounds impossible, but all the instruments agree that some form of higher technology was involved. Whatever it was, it was light-paces ahead of anything our scientists have ever come up with.'

And he explained to Keller what they had all seen.

When he had finished, Keller stood up, dusted himself down and faced the crowd of Cantorian survivors. There must have been at least a thousand of them gathered there, looking to him for leadership.

'Well? What are we waiting for? Let's go and check this place out!'

On a low flat plain on the unnamed new planet, the Aquanth contingent had landed in neat rows. Ayl had kept the ships' crews in telepathic contact, ensuring they all made it through the storm together.

All but one. Wan's ship had been caught in turbulence and spun off course, and Ayl couldn't make contact with his mind.

He tried not to worry about it. His people needed him now, especially with his mother still so weak. When Ayl had stepped down the ramp on to the ground of a new world, his mother's ship had already landed. Clouds of dust still seethed in the sky, but they were settling.

From behind him came the wheezes and gasps of Aquanths struggling to breathe in the dusty air. He could feel their panicked thoughts. *We'll die here. There's no water.*

'There *is* water here!' he told them firmly. 'The ship's computer confirmed it. We had to land the ships on solid ground, because it's safer. But we know there are seas on this new world. We'll reach them. Have faith.'

The rasps and wheezes slowly became less desperate, more even. Ayl turned away and looked up into the sky, praying for one more ship to emerge from the clouds.

Wan, can you hear me? Are you out there?

The sky remained empty.

Ayl looked down, overcome with sorrow. *I guess it was one miracle too many. We must give thanks for what we DO have. The Current of Life has spared so many of us. My people need me now. I can mourn my loss in private.*

A howl of engines broke his trance. Excited, he looked up and saw the last ship descending through the dust clouds. *They made it!* But he still couldn't contact Wan's mind and that troubled him. There could have been an accident, a collision . . .

It wasn't until Wan emerged from the landed ship, blinking in the strong light and coughing, that Ayl at last knew he was alive. *Now* he could sense Wan's thoughts! He embraced his friend, laughing in relief.

'Wan, what *happened* to you? I couldn't contact you, I tried so hard . . .'

'I passed out,' Wan admitted. 'When the turbulence hit, and we went into a spin . . . I was so scared, Ayl. I just fainted on the spot.' Wan clutched at his throat. 'Ayl, I can't breathe . . .'

'Yes you can,' Ayl assured him. 'Your body will adjust. You just have to trust it.' He patted Wan on the shoulder. 'Hey. I learned, didn't I? So it can't be too hard, can it?'

'Easy for you to say,' Wan gasped. 'How come you're the only one here not freaking out?'

He's right, Ayl thought. *These people are all terrified. I have to do something.*

So he walked among the Aquanths, and he spoke to them telepathically.

However bad this looks now, it's not the end of the world. It is the beginning of a new one. Everything that's happened today was prophesied, millions of turns ago. Don't be afraid. A higher power is at work here. The three worlds have become one. That was our destiny, laid down before the first Aquanth was born. We cannot change it, but we can change ourselves. We can adapt. And above all, we can do what Aquanths do best: pray, and keep faith.

He moved through the crowd, calming people, speaking to them. He didn't say much, but he didn't need to. Just a few gentle words made the difference.

He soon realized his calm was contagious. The people he left in his wake were no longer scared. They were uncertain of what the future would bring, but no longer afraid to look it in the eye.

I'm making a difference, Ayl thought happily to himself. *That's all I ever wanted, really.*

He opened his mind to his people, letting them all

share his inner peace. The Aquanths poured into his mind, drawing from his reassuring spirit as if it were a spring of fresh water. He had never felt so much at one with his people.

Thank you, he thought to the Current of Life and the Gods of Aquanthis. *Thank you for this gift.*

'We should pray together,' he said out loud. He had walked to the top of a little hill, and beneath him the Aquanths had gathered in silent rows. 'Our first prayer on this new world. We should give thanks and ask for guidance.'

There was no answer from his people except reverence.

Ayl wondered what he ought to say. None of the standard prayers seemed to fit; it wasn't every day that your world was destroyed, but your entire race survived. Oh well. He'd just have to make it up as he went along.

'Current of Life,' he began, 'we offer thanks. Our peoples have finally left the worlds they knew, and travelled to a new home . . .'

They weren't repeating his words. To his astonishment, he realized his people were not praying with him. They were murmuring in joy and awe, looking up at him as if he had been transformed.

243

Then one by one they bowed down.

Ayl looked to the crowd, to where his mother stood holding on to the Naptarch's arm for support. As the Aquanths bowed down, she bowed with them.

He was so shocked he stopped speaking. He glanced behind himself, but saw nothing there.

Mother, what's wrong? What is everyone bowing to?

She smiled. *Look at yourself, Ayl. Then you will understand.*

Ayl looked at his hands. They were radiating a glimmering blue light. His whole body was glowing, sparkling with divine radiance.

With shaking hands, Ayl's mother removed her ceremonial headdress and laid it down. 'And so, as the old world passes, a new one begins. Change and rebirth, for ever. So must it be.'

'So must it be,' the Aquanths echoed.

'You mean—'

She nodded. 'The Current of Life has chosen you, my son. My work is done. You are the high priest now.'

19

Keller paused for breath at the crest of a hill. 'OK, everyone. This looks like a good place to take a break.'

Thousands more Cantorians had joined them as they trekked across the dry land, emerging from other ships. Now they sat down on the ground together, sweaty and exhausted. Keller did the same. Hours of hiking in search of other survivors had left him bone-weary, but they had to carry on exploring.

'What I wouldn't give for a cool glass of lumojuice,' he said, squinting up at the sun.

'Yeah, well,' said the trader he'd arrested on the ship, who was now as free as all the rest. 'If you hadn't given all my merchandise away, I could sell you one, couldn't I?'

They glared at one another. Then, overcome by the absurdity of it, they both started to laugh.

It's a whole new world, Keller thought. There was a good view from up here. He gazed around in awe, letting his eyes drink in the sight: newly created mountain ranges, flat plains and a great ocean that stretched as far as the eye could see.

Something caught his eye in the far distance. A white spire, somehow still standing unbroken. To one side of it, empty plains; to the other, the sea.

Memory flooded back to him. *That spire cost a fortune. It's supposed to be completely indestructible. A monument built to outlast any disaster . . .*

He leapt to his feet. 'That's the Mausoleum of the Trade Kings!'

Tyrus followed his gaze. 'He's right! So that rubble all around it must be . . .'

'. . . what's left of the royal palace,' Yall finished.

Keller was already heading off down the hill towards it.

His hopes of finding any part of the palace still in one piece faded the closer he came. The entire complex had been crushed almost flat, like an elaborate sandcastle trampled by a spiteful child. Giant boulders – no doubt lumps of Bellus – lay half buried, and the stumps of a few marble pillars jutted up from the ocean of wreckage. Keller waded through splintery debris, recognizing fragments of ornate woodwork and antique furniture.

Eventually he discovered two huge double doors that had fallen. One was flat, the other lay at an angle like a ramp. He walked up it to overlook the destruction, thinking how strange it was to see the familiar carved wood under his boots.

I'm standing in what used to be the throne room. Portraits used to hang on the walls here. Now there aren't even any walls.

But there was a jutting piece of gilded wood among the debris, the corner of a picture frame. Curiosity nudged at him; he had to see what had survived.

He lowered himself down from the edge of the door and went to pull it out. The picture pulled free, the bottom half of the frame cracking off and hanging loose.

Keller looked down at his own face, staring pompously out from a piece of torn canvas. Behind him stood Trade King Lial, resplendent in his jewels and robes of office. He remembered posing for that picture – a real old-fashioned painting, not a holo-image. Not even a whole turn had passed since that day.

I hardly recognize myself any more.

He tossed the broken picture on to a pile of rubble without giving it a second thought. Calls from nearby told him the other Cantorian survivors had finally caught up.

Tyrus, once again, was the first to find him. 'Your Majesty? We need to continue the search for survivors, but if you wish to stay here, I'm sure the others will understand . . .'

'No,' Keller said. 'I'm done here. Let's go.'

They walked on and on, skirting the edge of the great ocean, climbing hills to get a better view. Nobody showed. In this great new planet, the Cantorians seemed completely alone. There was nothing for it but to head back to the ruined capital.

The sun had sunk low in the sky before Keller finally looked down from the remains of a city wall to see another group of people making their way towards them, less than half a kilopace away. His heart leaped as he saw they were wearing orange overalls. Although his throat was dry and painful, he yelled at the top of his voice for the others to come and see.

'Are they Cantorians?' Tyrus asked, squinting.

'No,' Keller grinned. 'Those, my old friend, are Bellori.'

'Without their armour?'

'Oh, yes. It comes off, you know.'

Tyrus's face went through several highly satisfying

contortions. 'But . . . but . . . they look so small!' he finally spluttered.

'You can't always judge by appearances,' Keller said. 'Pass me the holo-binox, would you? Let's see if I know any of this motley crowd . . .'

He focused the high-tech binoculars, zooming in on the party of Bellori. They looked just as dusty and weary as the Cantorians, but their faces were determined. Keller felt a flutter of excitement as he recognized some of the generals from Dray's flagship. If they had survived, could that mean . . . ?

He moved the binoculars around, afraid to hope for too much. And there she was, leading the group, fair hair blowing in the wind. Unbeaten, even after all she'd been through.

'Dray!' he yelled out loud. 'DRAY!'

Any other day, he could have played it cool. But not today. He jumped down from the wall and ran, sprinting across the ground to reach her.

'Someone's coming,' said General Vayne, shading his eyes. 'Not armed. Looks like a Cantorian.'

Dray frowned, then her eyes widened. Her heart skipped a beat. *Keller!*

Leaving her bewildered generals behind, she broke

into a run. She forgot how tired she was. She forgot everything else but the young man running to meet her.

They both ran madly towards each other. As they drew within a few paces of one another, they stopped in their tracks, uncertain what to do next.

Dray fidgeted, feeling awkward. Keller put his hands in his pockets.

'You're alive, then,' he said, grinning broadly.

'Looks that way, doesn't it?' Dray replied, beaming back at him. 'Did your people . . . ?'

'They're safe!' Keller burst out. 'Every single ship made it through. You guys and your safety features!' His face changed, became serious again. 'But what about you? Did you lose any people when . . . when Bellus blew up?'

Dray hung her head. 'There were casualties. We don't know how many yet. Some of the evacuation ships were hit. The speed those fragments were flying at – there was nothing the pilots could do.'

'I'm so sorry,' Keller said.

Dray nodded. 'Can you believe this planet? I have to keep pinching myself to check I'm not dreaming.'

Keller turned to look out over the plains below the ruins of his capital, and Dray came to stand by his side. 'It's impossible,' she said. 'All of this. You can't smash worlds together and get one big world. And the computers say there's life already!'

'Tyrus says some highly advanced technology was at work,' Keller said, shrugging. 'I guess Ayl would call it a higher power. Maybe they're the same thing.'

'Look at this,' Dray said. There was a tiny plant growing from the ground beneath them, no larger than her finger. Its leaves were bright red.

'New life,' Keller said. 'It's true, then. Accelerated evolution. Holy—'

The ground shook.

Dray yelled and grabbed hold of Keller, just as he caught hold of her. *It's only an aftershock*, she thought, as the earth bucked beneath her feet and they struggled to keep their balance. *Just the planet settling down.*

'It's an aftershock!' she shouted.

'I know!' Keller shouted back.

The tremors died away. Dray was still holding a fistful of Keller's shirt. He still had hold of her shoulder. His body felt warm against hers.

Very gently, he reached and brushed the hair out of her face. She looked up into his eyes. The intensely blue eyes of a young man, a boy no more.

He held her gaze for a long time. Then he touched

her face again, tenderly, and she moved hers up towards him.

'Keller! Dray!' The happy shout rang across the fields.

Dray jumped away as if she had been given an electric shock and smoothed down the front of her overalls.

Ayl waved crazily as he led a group of Aquanths towards them. 'I thought I'd never find you!'

Ayl held his friends in a tight embrace. He remembered the last time they'd held each other like this, looking down on Bellus, afraid they'd never see each other again. All around them, Cantorians, Aquanths and Bellori looked on, whispering between themselves. Many of them were smiling.

'I hate to say "I told you so",' he said with a grin. 'But you have to admit, three did become one. Just like I said.'

'Three planets, merged into one new planet,' agreed Dray. 'Too bad we can't talk to whoever made that prophecy of yours. It wasn't just a prophecy, was it?'

Ayl remembered how the tablet had blazed with uncanny light as the worlds rushed together. 'It was a gift,' he said. 'It turned a disaster into a new beginning.

Whoever created that artefact had abilities far beyond anything we know. It makes my telekinetic powers look like child's play.'

'Perhaps whoever made it is still out there, somewhere,' Dray mused.

Ayl looked to the skies, imagining what secrets still lay out there among the stars, waiting until the three races were wise enough to unlock them. 'Perhaps.'

'Well, our worlds have come together all right,' Keller said briskly. 'Now we have to make sure our people do the same.'

Ayl smiled. 'And that's the real challenge, isn't it?'

Keller laughed. 'OK. I'm sorry I ever doubted you, Blue. I admit it, you've been right almost every time.'

'So, Ayl . . . what *else* does the prophecy say?' Dray asked. 'It can't just stop at "three become one", can it? What happens next?'

'That part is up to us,' Ayl said. 'All three of our peoples, acting together.' He paused. 'I've got some ideas . . . if you'd like to hear them?'

Keller shrugged. 'Sure. I mean, I haven't got any urgent appointments right now. Dray?'

'Go on, Blue. We're listening.'

'I think we should call our new home planet Trinity,' Ayl said. 'And make a pact, right here and now, to work together. We share the resources, we share the work. All three peoples are equal, united, now and forever. Deal?'

'Deal,' said Dray and Keller at the same time. They shook hands on it.

Onlookers in the crowd surrounding them muttered excitedly. They took pictures and wrote down what had been said. 'History in the making,' Ayl heard one of the Cantorians say.

Ayl had a sudden, clear vision of the future. He saw a great portrait of the three of them standing together making this agreement, hanging in a majestic building with a plaque beneath it . . . and then it was gone.

'Well, now we've settled that,' he said, 'there's something urgent I need to ask. We desperately need to find water. Have either of you seen any?'

'You're in luck!' Dray said. 'We're right next to the sea. It's just beyond the ruins. Head for the white spire and keep going.'

'You can't miss it,' Keller shouted after Ayl as he ran joyously up the side of the hill. 'It's the big blue wet thing!'

Ayl ran through the ruins of the Cantorian capital, leaping from stone to stone on his webbed feet. At last he saw the sea, shimmering at the edge of the ruins.

He reached the water's edge and dived in without stopping. One after another, his fellow Aquanths dived in after him, united in absolute bliss. Above their plunging bodies, the sun slowly set on the planet called Trinity for the first time.

20

Campfires had been lit in the ruins of Cantor's old capital, now renamed 'Foundation City'. A Cantorian had suggested it as a joke, and the name had stuck. Foraging groups had dug preserved foodstuffs out of the debris of shops, and there was plenty to go around, for now.

By the firelight in the old central plaza, General Dray called her troops to order. She explained what the three leaders had agreed, and what the future would hold for Trinity.

'I'm sure some of you have things to say to me,' she concluded. 'Now's the time. Speak.'

'General, with respect, we're not farmers,' one warrior said. 'I can plant mines. I don't know how to plant corn.'

'We're not fish, either,' groused another. 'So what's this new world got to offer us, eh? What are we meant to *do* here?'

'We are no longer on Bellus,' Dray said. 'But we can still be warriors. *If* we choose to.'

'How do you mean, *choose?*' the warrior said 'What else are Bellori good for but fighting?'

'That may have been true on our old home, but it doesn't have to be that way now.' Dray took a deep breath. 'Bellus doesn't need her children to defend her any more. For better or worse, that duty has been taken from us. We're free. We can change.'

'What if we don't want to change?' an angry voice cried out.

'Then Trinity will always have room for those who choose to defend her!' Dray said. 'We will always need warriors!' She struck the top of an empty food crate, making it boom like a drum. 'But before we defend this world, we must make it safe.'

Muttering broke out among the crowd. Bellori looked to one another, wondering what enemy Dray was talking about. 'Safe from what?' one soldier finally asked.

'Look around you,' she said. 'Look at the ruins you're standing in. Is this a fit place for families to live? We Bellori have always been proud of our strength. Well, now we're going to prove how strong we are. We're going to help rebuild this place.' She stood.

'Listen up, all of you! Priority one is to clear the ruins of Foundation City and make them safe for habitation! Commanders, deploy your troops by city zone. I want the first families able to settle here by noon tomorrow. MOVE!'

Immediately, the Bellori went to work. Squads moved out to form digging parties, planning how to remove blockages from roads and empty rubble from the less damaged houses. Not a single voice was raised in protest.

Dray smacked dust from her hands, satisfied.

She crossed the plaza to where a group of warriors was standing around a fallen beam. 'Let me show you how this is done,' she said. She bent down, gripped it tightly and began to drag it away.

On a raised stone platform not far from Dray's plaza, Keller and his Trade Council surveyed the wreckage of Cantor's capital. The platform had once held a group of dancing statues, Keller remembered. Now there was only one sad-looking marble foot, broken off at the ankle.

'It's all gone,' moaned a merchant who had said very little else for the past hour. He kept looking morosely over the edge as if he meant to jump. 'All of it. Smashed to bits. Destroyed.'

Keller wished he'd shut up, but then the rest of the Trade Council weren't exactly happy about things either, and to be honest he could hardly blame them. They *had* lost everything.

'None of you had all your investments here, did you?' said Tyrus. 'You all had offworld bank accounts, I trust?'

'Yes, thank the fates,' muttered a trader.

'I had eight tonnes of gold in a satellite vault,' groaned the forlorn merchant. 'It's gone now, disappeared . . . must have fallen from orbit . . . maybe it's somewhere out there, under the sea . . .'

'Got any more happy thoughts, Tyrus?' Yall snapped. 'Why don't you tell us all to collect on our insurance?'

'There *is* a positive side to this,' Keller insisted. 'Think about the rebuilding. Think about the infrastructure! Krack, think about the property deals! You do realize that this world is *three times* the size of the old one?'

'That's a lot of real estate!' pondered one of the councillors.

'Remember all those metals and minerals under the surface of Bellus?' Keller added. 'All that quantanium ore that the Bellori would never let us extract?'

'By the belly of King Wantis,' breathed Yall. 'Of course. Bellus exploded. The ore has mined *itself*.'

'Exactly!' Keller said. 'And where did it go? It's lying around out there, literally fallen from the sky in chunks! And if that's on the surface of our world, what's beneath? Think about the mining rights, gentlemen.'

The Trade Council fell silent, but it was no longer mournful silence. Keller could tell what was going on inside those minds. They were calculating, projecting, making business plans.

He had their attention. Now he just had to milk it for all it was worth.

'Of course, the main trouble with Cantor was how little water we had,' he remarked. 'I guess we don't need to buy water from Aquanthis any more, do we? Not now the entire planet is here.'

'Agriculture!' exploded Tyrus. 'The boy's right! We can irrigate the whole planet, make full use of the fertile ground to grow crops!'

Yall cut in: 'And that's not even counting hydroponics . . .'

'. . . or orbital facilities . . .'

'. . . or livestock . . .'

'. . . or *underwater* cultivation complexes! Think of it, Your Majesty! The profit margins could be beyond anything Cantor has ever known!'

'Cantor is *gone*,' Keller reminded them. 'And we're going to need to share those resources, not hoard them for ourselves. That goes for trading, too. Oh, we can still barter and trade, just like we always have. But if we make a profit, we do it for our entire people.'

'Our people?' Yall was flummoxed. 'But if we're not Cantorians, then who are we?'

'There are no Cantorians, Bellori or Aquanths any more. We're all one people. The Trinitarians.'

'But we can rebuild Cantor, you said it yourself—'

'No!' *I have to get this through to them if it kills me*, Keller thought desperately. 'How many times? This is *not* about rebuilding Cantor. We have to build a new world. A better world.'

Ayl swam over the drowned ruins of a Cantorian suburb, heading back to the dry land. His people followed behind him, leaving silver wakes in the starlight. They stepped out of the waves, walking upright on to the shore.

He smiled as he saw the Cantorians and Bellori had gathered on the beach to meet them. Many of them carried flaming torches. *New light in the darkness*, Ayl thought. *And they brought it here themselves.*

'I hadn't planned for a ceremony,' he told his mother, 'but this is starting to feel like one.'

'Maybe it should be,' she said. A twinkle Ayl hadn't seen for far too long had come back into her eyes, now she had laid her burden of rulership down. 'Your people seem ready.'

'I suppose. Would you lead us in prayer, then?'

She tutted and smiled, shaking her head. 'You're the high priest now, Ayl. You'd better get used to it.'

'Well, I'll try. But I could never replace you.'

She looked at him, her deep blue eyes very grave. 'Me? I barely did anything, my son. It was you, alone out of all of us, who understood the prophecy and led us to salvation. You are the pathfinder who will lead the way in this new world, not I. From now on, it is I who will listen while you speak.' She laid a hand on his shoulder. 'Your time has come. Embrace it.'

Ayl looked along the beach. The Aquanths had sat down cross-legged on the sand, and the Cantorians and Bellori came to sit with them. They were all waiting patiently for him to begin.

Between land and sea, he thought, *by the light of the*

torches. Earth, water and fire. Once again, three come together as one. This is the right place.

Ayl's skin began to glow blue, casting a pool of light first around his feet, then brightening to illuminate the whole beach. He heard the assembled crowd gasping in wonder.

Still he hesitated, unsure of what he ought to say.

He turned his eyes up to the night sky, to where the first faint stars were coming out. And from the deep blackness between the stars, he seemed to hear a distant whisper, a voice somehow both old and young: *Finish the prayer.*

He smiled. Of course – he had begun to pray, but had never finished.

He raised his hands to the sky.

'Current of Life, we offer thanks. For our peoples have finally left the worlds they knew, and travelled to a new home among the stars. Bless us as we take our first steps on to this new world, and grant us the wisdom to care for it. From the fires of destruction, let us forge peace. Let us go forward into the future as friends. This day we are united – and may nothing divide us ever again: for in peace and joy, three have become one.'

All the way along the beach, the words were

repeated. 'Three have become one,' chanted people who had once been Cantorians, Aquanths and Bellori. Some voices were harsh and roaring, some were clear and bright, and some were soft and breathy as gentle waves, but all were strong. And together they rose up as one voice, above a landscape torn and littered with wreckage and devastation.

Dray and Keller came and stood beside Ayl. Together, the three leaders of Trinity looked on their people, and their hearts filled with pride.

Epilogue

The planet known as Trinity was coming to the end of its first turn around the sun. From a high orbit, it looked much the same as before. But a closer scan would reveal new structures on its surface where only ruin and devastation had been.

Cities and settlements had sprung up, linked by a faint network of roads. A steady stream of cargo ships, bringing supplies in and ferrying trade goods out to distant systems, passed around the planet like a fine silver chain.

Much of the planet was golden and green now, where previously it had been red-brown and barren. Crops were flourishing in the fertile soil, fed by a tracery of irrigation pipes. Markets bustled in the towns, with busy merchants haggling over grain and comparing ingots of rare metals.

The waters of Trinity were alive with laughter. Graceful figures swam in the seas, and even ventured deep inland, following the courses of rivers to visit distant friends. Glowing structures pulsed from deep under the ocean; deep caverns echoed with thankful hymns of praise.

But in an infinite universe, many things may exist. Space is deep, and holds many secrets – some that are best left uncovered. And so, high on their guard towers, stern-faced sentinels ensured their weapons were close at hand and kept vigil.

Watching the skies. Waiting. Protecting Trinity from the unknown.

Trinity: 20 years on . . .

Trinity is a medium-sized habitable planet measuring 5,237 killipaces across. It is located 97 million killipaces from its sun, and 18,000 light-turns from the Milky Way galaxy. Trinity is sometimes referred to as the 'Big Three'. It has an estimated population of 4.7 million. The planet's official bird is the falchort. Trinity's flag features three interlinking circles on a blue background.

History

Trinity was formed twenty turns ago, following catastrophic explosions on the surface of Bellus during an invasion by a Nara-Karith army. The eruptions created a gravitational force that caused the three planets in the Trinity System – Aquanthis, Bellus and Cantor – to collide. The resulting land-mass, now called Trinity, fulfilled an ancient prophesy predicted that their three peoples would become one.

Geography

The capital city of Trinity is called Foundation City, where the Palace of Freedom and other government buildings are located. 50% of Trinity's surface is water, with about one third of the population living in watery regions. 40% of Trinity's soil is arable. Trinity's temperate climate, mild winters and abundant water supplies provide ideal conditions for agriculture. To the north of the country are rugged mountains, formed from volcanic Bellori rock. The harsh Zarix desert is found in the southern hemisphere of Trinity. Trinity has frequent low-magnitude earthquakes, as its plates are still shifting. Thus most of Trinity's buildings are constructed from reinforced plasteel.

Politics

Trinity is a constitutional monarchy. Its head of state is King Keller (formerly Trade King Keller), but the planet is governed by elected counselors. The government is bound by a constitution that was drafted by the planet's three founders: Keller, Dray and Ayl. This constitution grants Trinity's citizens rights such as freedom, equality, solidarity and justice. Elections occur every three years.

Economy

Trinity's unit of currency is the credit. Trinity is one of the fastest-growing economies in the universe, with gross domestic product growing at a rate of 9.7% each turn. Agriculture represents 30% of Trinity's economy, with manufacturing (18%), retail (16%), mining (18%) and defence contracting (20%) being the next largest industries. Although still small, one of Trinity's fastest growing industries is tourism, as visitors from other planets tour the planet's natural wonders and impressive new cities.

Demographics

Trinity is a multi-cultural society. 25% of the population is of Cantorian descent; 23% is of Bellori origin, and 27% is of Aquanth extraction. A further 19% of the population have mixed heritage, with intermarriages becoming increasingly common following the marriage of General Dray and King Keller. Trinity also welcomes immigrants, with approximately 6% of its population coming from other planets.

Religion

Trinity is a religiously tolerant planet, with Aquanth spirituality being the predominant faith practised. Observers take part in rituals such as meditation, mind-sharing and chanting. The head of the church is High Priest Ayl. His teachings have deviated from the traditional emphasis on conformity and made individuality acceptable to his followers. He has also introduced outreach programmes, which minister to the sick and needy. Approximately 80% of Trinity's population attend temple services.

Languages

A common language called Trinitin is spoken on Trinity. Although Aquanthis, Bellus and Cantor originally had their own languages, the proto-Aquanth, ancient Bellori and pre-Cantorian dialects had fallen out of usage many thousands of turns before the planets merged. The few surviving tablets written in these ancient languages are housed in the Lady Moa Memorial Library.

Culture

Martial arts are popular on Trinity. Bellori combat methods are practised recreationally, with public competitions are held in sporting arenas. Spacecraft racing is also widely enjoyed, with the annual Trinity Derby a highlight of the sporting calendar. Prince Iccus is the current winner of the prestigious King Lial Cup. With an abundance of warm, clean water on Trinity, swimming is another common leisure activity.

The most important public holiday is a three-day celebration marking the creation of Trinity. On the first day, the children of Trinity dress up as Nara-Karith and take to the streets to frighten grown-ups in exchange for goodies. The following day there are firework displays, to commemorate the eruption of Bellus, with feasts, dancing and drinking of samthorn wine. It is traditional to attend temple on the third day, to give thanks for Trinity's creation.

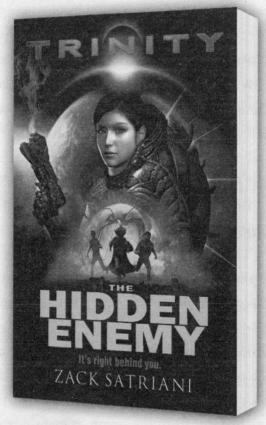

Prologue

The rock drifted silently through space.

It had travelled an unknowable distance through the emptiness of the universe. For billions of years it had journeyed, crossing the grand sweep of galaxies and the immense nothingness between them. Centuries had passed since the rock last felt the pull of gravity.

But now it was drawn to a small yellow star, surrounded by three planets.

The first of the three worlds shone like a blue pearl in the darkness of space. No land showed anywhere on the perfect globe, just an endless expanse of water. A pair of titanic sea creatures, large enough to be seen from thousands of paces, gently broke the surface of the ocean-world before returning to the depths. As the rock passed, a billion living minds, all joined as one, reached out from the ocean in joyous greeting.

The rock moved on, silent.

Next it passed a large, craggy planet, pitted and

scarred by a thousand ancient volcanoes. But, though the landscape seemed lifeless, there were still signs of civilization. High-powered targeting lasers from a dozen weapon systems locked on the rock, alert for any danger. But there was no evidence of a threat, so the planet's guns remained still.

The rock continued on, as gravity tugged on its massive bulk.

It curved round the third planet. Life swarmed in a patchwork of forests and fields. On the night-side, the lights of great cities shone like a galaxy of stars. Around the planet spun hundreds of artificial moons – satellites that swept the rock with scanners, calculating its worth.

The rock moved past the verdant planet, then began its orbit around the star once more.

And deep beneath the surface, something stirred.

1

'It's not a bad deal you've put together there, lad,' said Tyrus, leaning back in his seat and scratching his thick, grey beard. 'I never thought I'd say this, but all right – I'll lease you the ships.'

Keller eyed him steadily. 'You won't regret it, Tyrus. Your share of the profits should be a tidy sum, once it's all up and running. I just need your print on the contract . . .'

He pushed the data-slate across the dark oak table to the older man, and held his breath. Every eye in the vaulted chamber was on him, from the life-size portraits of long-dead traders staring down from the walls, to the scrum of assistants, advisors and hangers-on standing either side of the long table, tracking the deal. Even though he couldn't see him, Keller knew his father was there too, watching. He recognized the particular hush that fell over a room whenever Cantor's trade king was present.

Tyrus picked up the slate and scanned through it one last time.

Come on, you avaricious old crow, thought Keller, his heart pounding. *Make the deal . . .*

The old man looked up into the teenager's eyes, as if to weigh his value. Then, without breaking eye contact, he pressed his thumb firmly on the contract. A cheer went up around the room as Tyrus passed the data-slate back to Keller.

'But I'm afraid your terms were far too generous, My Prince,' he said, a patronizing smile on his wrinkled face. 'You should have looked more closely at the space-harbour charges. They're all coming out of your share.'

Keller chuckled. 'Is that so, Tyrus? Then you're right, I should have looked more closely.' His shoulders shook, as the chuckle turned into a belly laugh.

The older man's eyes narrowed. 'I'm glad you think losing four thousand credits per turn is so amusing.'

'Oh, I'm not laughing about that,' replied Keller, wiping his streaming eyes.

'Then what *are* you laughing about?' Tyrus folded his arms, as he waited to hear the joke.

'You were so busy trying to fleece me on the space-harbour charges that you weren't paying attention to the maintenance estimates,' said Keller, grinning. 'They leave you paying all the costs while I take all the profits!'

'You *cheated* me?' roared Tyrus, standing so quickly his antique chair flew backwards. 'I'll have you in the Commerce Courts faster than you can say "breach of contract"!'

'Sit down, sit down,' said Keller, waving his hand. 'I haven't sealed the contract. It was never meant to be a real deal anyway. Why would I want ten of your rickety old space-hulks? Everyone knows they can hardly make it out of the system without breaking down. No, I just bet my friends that I could hire half of your fleet – and that you'd pay me for it too!'

As he spoke, Keller's friends crowded round, all trying to slap him on the back.

'Why you cocky little—' Tyrus stopped in mid-flow as a tall figure stepped out of the throng. Biting his lip, the old trader bowed. 'Your Majesty.'

'Don't worry, my friend,' said Trade King Lial, his deep voice carrying across the room. 'I will speak to my son about the importance of respect in negotiations. Keller, walk with me a moment.'

'Of course, Sire,' said Keller, following his father

out of the palace's trade chamber and through an archway.

They walked slowly along a balcony overlooking the palace gardens. Keller let his gaze wander across the landscape. Plants from all reaches of the galaxy flourished in the rich soil, and the sweet, spicy scent of flowering Circian orchids filled the air. To their left, alcoves in the wall held sculptures and statues from dozens of different worlds.

The gardens are a paradise, thought Keller. And well they should be – they'd cost enough.

'I don't understand why you waste your talents with such games.' King Lial sighed. 'If you made deals like that for real, you'd be a wealthy man in your own right by now.'

'What do I need money for?' Keller laughed. 'I'm a prince, and one day I'll be King of Cantor!'

'*Trade* King,' Lial snapped, a note of irritation entering his voice. 'A working king, a respected merchant who protects Cantorian interests in the intergalactic community! Believe me, you'll need men like Tyrus by your side then.'

Lial turned to his son and Keller looked back into his face. There could never be any doubt that they were father and son. The young prince had the same strong jaw and sharp nose as his father, but where Keller's hair was jet black, Lial's was now pure white. The older man's skin seemed dry and thin, and creases and wrinkles spread out from his eyes and the sides of his mouth when he talked.

How old is he now? Keller wondered. *Eighty turns? Ninety?*

'It was a good trick, father,' said Keller, risking a smile.

'That it was,' said Lial, an identical grin spreading across his face. 'The look on that old skinflint's face . . .' He slapped his son on the shoulder and the pair started walking again. 'But we have something serious to talk about. This morning I received a com from General Iccus.'

Keller curled his lip. 'The Bellori leader?'

Lial nodded. 'It's about the asteroid.'

'Surely they must have seen sense by now?'

'Quite the contrary. The Bellori are refusing to consider any mining activity.'

'The mullocks,' growled Keller. 'Don't they realize the value of the detrillium in that rock?'

'Their priorities are different to ours. They want to use it as a military base.'

Keller ground his teeth in frustration. 'Can't they

see that if we mine it, we'll *all* get rich and then they can buy as many warships as they like?'

'It seems not.' King Lial shrugged. 'Anyway, the Bellori aren't our only problem. The Aquanths are claiming that the asteroid is sacred.'

Keller's eyes bulged. 'You *are* joking?'

'I wish I was.'

'But that's . . . that's . . . that's just the craziest thing I've ever heard,' spluttered Keller. 'How can a floating lump of space-rock be *holy*?'

'Lady Moa says that it is the "Heavenly Messenger" mentioned in their prophecies. Apparently, its arrival marks a new era of cooperation and harmony between our three planets.'

Keller shook his head. 'That high priestess has been living under the sea for too long. *A new era of cooperation and harmony . . .*'

'Well there's no sign of it so far,' said King Lial. 'None of us seem willing to budge.'

'So what happens now?'

'I've suggested a meeting – a conference of the three leaders to discuss how to proceed.'

'When are they coming?' Keller asked, making a mental note to be away at the time. It would be just his luck to get caught up in all the tedious politics.

'That's the problem,' replied the trade king with a grimace. 'They aren't.'

'What do you mean?'

'Iccus won't agree to meet anywhere other than on the asteroid itself. It's the only place the Bellori consider neutral ground.'

'Mullocks,' muttered Keller again.

'Perhaps,' said his father. 'But we can't risk offending them, or trade in the Trinity System will be affected, and then we all pay.'

Keller frowned. 'Why are you telling me all this anyway?'

'Because you'll be joining me as part of the Cantorian delegation.'

'What?' Keller's face fell. 'But the Kaloon Derby is in three cycles,' he protested. He could already picture the after-party . . .

'This is state business,' Lial said firmly, clapping a strong hand down on his son's shoulder. 'And that comes before pleasure. It's time for you to learn about real negotiations . . .'